KILL SIGNS 2

ERNEST MORRIS

GOOD 2 GO PUBLISHING

KILLING SIGNS
Written by Ernest Morris
Cover Design: Davida Baldwin, Odd Ball Designs
Typesetter: Mychea
ISBN: 978-1-947340-48-0
Copyright © 2020 Good2Go Publishing
Published 2020 by Good2Go Publishing
7311 W. Glass Lane • Laveen, AZ 85339
www.good2gopublishing.com
https://twitter.com/good2gobooks
G2G@good2gopublishing.com
www.facebook.com/good2gopublishing
www.instagram.com/good2gopublishing

ACKNOWLEDGMENTS

First Let Me Begin by thanking the man above for helping me understand how valuable talent is and that it shouldn't be wasted. It took me a while, but I now understand my worth. Every day I try to make a difference in this world, and as hard as it is to make a breakthrough, I finally feel like it's about to pay off. If I can show one person how important life is, then I have done my job.

I would like to thank everyone at GOOD2GO PUBLISHING for continuing to see the best in me. Even when I was at a low point in my life, you continued to trust me. It's because of you that I can walk around and be proud of my success.

There are many obstacles that we will face during our time on earth, but never back down, and most importantly, never give up.

Finally, I want to thank you, the reader, for continuing to support us by buying our novels. Without you, we as authors wouldn't have a career. You make it possible for us to continue expressing our visions through writing. Look out for my new novel, *Breaking the Chains*, coming soon. Enjoy!!

DEDICATIONS

I Dedicate This Book to everyone out there struggling to make ends meet. I'm the perfect example that if you put your mind to it, you can do or be anything you want. Don't let anyone tell you that you can't.

I want to dedicate this to all my family and friends. Chubb, Walid, Le'Shea, Sahmeer, Demina, Shayana, Nakisha, Brandi, Mina, Kendra, Rasheed, Maurice, Theresa, Dwunna, Kimmy, Leneek, Ci Ci, Gianni, Catrena, Sherry, Trevor, Brandon, Ty, Stud, Yaya, Ru, Lepo, Rich, No No, Bruce, LR, Ro, Sam, Doc, Love, Qua, Miz, Melo, Trizz, Kenya, Niema, Melissa, Samad, Michael, Yola, Anna, Anaya, Alyiah, Helena (CYN), Candy, Liz, Kayley, Monique, Nasira, Quill, Tamara, Ed, Shamika, Torey, Umar, Shirley, Amy, Susan, Sharon, Crystal, Champ, Luke, William, Tiffany, and there's so many more that I forgot to mention, but you know who you are. Stay positive and keep striving.

Well here we go again. Let's get it!!!!

PROLOGUE

"Tell me what you want, Ashley."

"You." She gasped.

"Where?"

"Bed."

He broke free, scooping her into his arms, and carried her quickly and seemingly without any strain into her bedroom. Sitting her on her feet beside the bed, he leaned down to switch on the bedside lamp. He glanced around the room and hastily closed the curtains.

"Don't worry, my sister is out of town for the weekend, and I'm quite sure she wouldn't mind this," Ashley chuckled.

"I'm not worried at all," Eric said softly. "Now what?"

"Make love to me."

"How?" he teased. "You have to tell me."

"For starters, you can undress me."

He smiled and stuck his index finger into her open shirt, pulling her toward him, then slowly unbuttoned her blouse. Tentatively she put her hands on his arms to steady herself. He didn't complain one bit. In fact, ever since he had that threesome with her and Veronica, he had wanted some more. Guess you could say that Ashley really had that good-good.

When he finished with the buttons, he pulled her shirt off and let it fall to the floor. Eric reached down to the waistband of her jeans, popped the button, and pulled down the zipper.

"Tell me what you want me to do to you, Ashley." His eyes smoldered, and his lips parted as he took quick, shallow breaths.

"Kiss me from here to here," she whispered, trailing her finger from the base of her ear, down her throat. He smoothed her hair out of the line of fire and bent, leaving sweet soft kisses along the path her finger was taking and back again.

"Now what?"

"My jeans and panties," Ashley murmured. Eric smiled, dropping to his knees in front of her. It felt so good to her. Hooking his thumbs into her jeans, he gently pulled them, along with her panties, down her legs. Ashley stepped out of them, leaving her with only a bra on.

"Now what, Ash?" He stopped and looked up

at her expectantly, but didn't get up.

"Kiss me," she whispered.

"Where?"

"You know where," she moaned, acting like she was a shy girl.

She pointed at the apex of her thighs, and he grinned wickedly. Ashley closed her eyes, mortified, but at the same time horny as fuck.

"Oh, with pleasure, my dear," he chuckled. Eric kissed her and unleashed his tongue, his long and thick tongue. She groaned every time his tongue touched her body. He didn't stop though, as his tongue circled her clitoris, driving her insane. It kept going around and around, up and down.

"Eric, please," she begged, not wanting to cum standing. She didn't have the strength to hold on any longer. "I want to fuck right now."

He stood up, his lips glistening with the evidence of her arousal. Ashley started pulling off his clothes as he fondled her breasts. She dropped to her knees in front of him, yanking down his boxers. His ten-inch python sprang free from its captor. Eric watched as she took hold of him, squeezing tightly. He groaned and tensed up when she took him into her mouth, sucking and licking every inch. He cupped her head tenderly, and she pushed him deeper into her mouth, pressing her lips together as tightly as she could.

"Fuck," he hissed through gritted teeth. "Ash, you made your point, I don't want to cum in your mouth."

She did it once more, and Eric bent down, grabbing her by the shoulder, and pulled her up to her feet, then tossed her on the bed. Ashley lay down, gazing up at him as he slowly positioned himself over her, licking his lips. He tore off her bra and kissed each of her breasts, teasing her nipples along the way. Gazing at her, he pushed her legs apart and slowly entered her steaming hot love box at a slow pace before speeding up.

"Faster, Eric, harder, yes, just like that," she moaned, lifting her body in the air, giving him more access to drill her.

He gazed down at her in triumph, kissing her hard, then really started to dig into her walls. Her orgasm was building at a rapid pace. Her legs tensed up beneath him.

"Come on, baby," he gasped. "Give it to me."

His words were what made her explode, magnificently, mind-numbingly, into a million pieces all over him, and he followed up with his own explosion.

"Ash! Oh fuck, Ash!" He collapsed on top of her with his head buried in her neck. "Damn, your pussy is so fucking good. I can get used to this."

"What would my sister think if she heard you talking about my kitty kat like that?" Ashley joked. They both burst out laughing as Eric rolled off of her.

He was looking up at the ceiling when his cell phone went off. Already knowing who it was from the ringtone, he let it go straight to voicemail. Seconds later, it went off again.

"Somebody's trying to get in touch with you. You better get that."

"It's just work," Eric replied, rubbing her pussy. It instantly got moist again from his touch. She was ready for action again, until the phone went off again. This time he knew something was wrong because Sonya would never call continuously like that. "Excuse me for a minute. Hello, Eric here."

"We have a major problem."

"What's wrong?" he asked, getting out of the bed.

"ADA Bachman hasn't been answering his phone for two days. Cynthia sent someone to his home, and they found his whole family murdered, including him. Eric, there was another horoscope quote written on his chest. I think we may have passed judgment on the wrong person. Our killer is still out there . . ."

CHAPTER ONE

The Hunter Becomes the Hunted

"**OPEN UP, OR WE'LL** kick down this door," the officer called out.

It is no exaggeration to say that my whole family was about to get a wake-up call from hell. All I was thinking at that particular moment was that the police could not kick down the door. This was the state of Ohio. We could get evicted for allowing someone to disturb the peace. I quickly unlatched the chain and swung the door open. I had on my dinosaur pajamas.

"What's your name?" the bearish-looking officer asked.

"Kerruche Brown."

"Where are your parents, Ms. Brown?"

"In bed. I'll go let them know that you need to talk to them."

"We'll go with you," said Officer Mylenski.

The officer's grim expression told me that it was not a request. I turned on the lights as we headed toward my parents' bedroom. I climbed the steps, thinking about how my parents were going to kill me for bringing these men upstairs, when suddenly both cops pushed rudely past me. By the time I had reached my parents' room, the overhead light was on and the cops were bending over my parents' bed.

Even with the two officers in the way, I could see that my mother and father looked all wrong. Their sheets and blankets were on the floor, and their nightclothes were bunched under their arms as if they'd tried to take them off. My father's arm looked like it had been twisted out of its socket. My mother was lying face down across her husband's body, and her tongue was sticking out of her mouth. It had turned black. I didn't need a coroner to tell me that they were both dead.

I knew it just moments after I saw them. I tried to rush toward them, but one of the officers stopped me in my tracks. He escorted me out of the room, putting his big paw hands on my shoulders so I couldn't break free.

"Mommy, Daddy, noooooo!"

"I'm sorry to do this," he said, shutting the door.

I didn't try to open it. I just stood there. Motionless. Almost not breathing. So you might be wondering why I wasn't bawling, or passing out from shock and horror. Or why I wasn't running to the bathroom to vomit or curling up in the fetal position, hugging my knees and sobbing. Or doing any of the things that a teenage girl who's just seen her murdered parents' bodies ought to do.

The answer is complicated, but here's the simplest way to say it. I'm not a whole lot like most girls. At least, not from what I can tell. For me, having a meltdown was seriously out of the question. When I called out to my parents a minute ago, that was me trying to show compassion.

From the time I was two, when I first started speaking in paragraphs that began with topic sentences, my father had told me that I was exceptionally smart. Later he told me that I was analytical and focused and that my detachment from watery emotion was a superb trait. He said that if I nurtured these qualities, I would achieve or even exceed my extraordinary potential, and this wasn't just a good thing, but a great thing. It would help my transitional way of thinking later on in life when my world would turn upside down. That's why I was more prepared for this catastrophe than most kids my age would be, or maybe any kids my age.

I went back downstairs and got my phone. I called my uncle and our family lawyer. I then went to my little brother's room and somehow told him the inexpressibly horrible news that our mother and father were dead, and that it was possible they'd been murdered.

"I want Mommy, Kerruche," he sobbed, holding on to my leg.

"It will be okay, Sahmeer, I promise."

After I completed that horrible task, perhaps the worst of my life, I tried to focus my fractured attention back on the huge officer that was standing there towering over me. He was a rough-looking character, like the bad cop in that show on FX's, *Snowfall*, who didn't like drug dealers.

Sergeant Puto was his name. He looked to be about thirty-six years old and in good physical condition. He had one continuous eyebrow, a furry ledge over his stony black eyes. His thin lips were set in a short, hard line, and the sleeves of his uniform were rolled up to his elbows. I noticed a zodiac sign tattooed on his wrist. It was the sign of the Gemini, which was my sign. Our birthdays must be in the same month, I thought.

The other officer, Officer McCown, was an entirely different guy. He had a basically pleasant, faintly lined face and wore a wedding ring, a CPD windbreaker, and steel-tipped boots. He looked sympathetic to us kids, sitting on the couch, waiting for the crime lab and coroner's office to arrive. He wasn't the one in charge, but his demeanor said something totally different.

Officer McCown stood with his back to us, talking on the phone to the Homicide Unit. After he ended the call, he looked around the room with his mouth wide open. I guess he couldn't believe how we lived, and I can't say I blame him. My parents weren't rich, but we lived as comfortably as most rich people. When he finished taking in the décor, he got down to business.

"Your parents were murdered sometime

during the night. We received a phone call from a neighbor about a disturbance at this address. That is why we are here. That faint odor you're smelling is coming from your parents' room. Once the detectives get here, they can determine the time and cause of death."

"My uncle is on his way here now," I told him. I had seen on television that when something happens to little kids, like losing their parents, the children end up in some foster care, separated from each other. My brother was all I had, and I'd be damned if I was going to lose him to the system.

"Stay here with them while I look around to make sure no one else is here," Puto said. As he walked away, I continued staring at his tattoo. For some strange reason, I was intrigued by it.

"Hello, everyone," a man wearing plainclothes said, walking into the apartment, followed by another man that looked almost as young as me. I knew they were cops from the guns on their hips and the badges that hung from their necks. "This penthouse is a crime scene. It's off-limits until I say otherwise. Are we

6

clear?"

I was still trying to process the fact that my parents were gone and my brother and I were temporary orphans. What really bothered me the most was the fact that I wasn't feeling remorseful. In fact, you may as well know, I am the reason they are dead. My mother was like a perpetual motion machine, never stopping, hardly sleeping at all. She seemed to barely notice people, even her own children. Her strength was in analyzing financial markets and managing other people's money.

My father co-owned a pharmaceutical company with a couple of his high school buddies. He was a chemist with a gigantic brain and enormous gifts. Unlike my mother, my dad engaged with us so intensely that after a few minutes of contact with him, I felt invaded to the core. Whenever my mother would be out late, he would come into my room and lie in bed with me. I could feel a part of his body that should never touch me, poking me from behind. I would pretend to be asleep while his hands freely roamed all over me. He never penetrated any parts of my body, but it felt like it. My mother

7

never once believed me when I said something. Tonight was the final straw when he came in drunk from losing a big investment deal that would have put his company over the top. He walked into the bathroom while I was in the shower, pulled out his penis, and pissed right in front of me. Once he was finished, he turned to me and started jerking off while staring at my naked body. I quickly grabbed a towel to cover myself and rushed out of there.

After getting dressed, I went to the kitchen to make a sandwich. He had a bottle of liquor sitting on the table with two glasses.

"You'll never touch me again," I mumbled to myself as tears escaped my eyes for the first time in my life since I was a baby. It would be the last time too!

I opened the cabinet that held the cleaning supplies, and mixed together a concoction, then inserted it into the bottle of liquor. I quickly rushed back to my room so I didn't get caught. An hour later, they were in their room arguing loudly and drinking. Then I heard a commotion and a loud thump, and then silence filled the air. I went to sleep with a smile on my face, until the loud banging on the door.

"Of course, Officer," I finally responded to his demand, snapping out of my daydream. "We wouldn't want to interfere in your very thorough investigation."

The medical examiner arrived at the same time as my uncle and the family lawyer. They all walked in at the same time. The lawyer and my uncle talked to the detectives while we sat there watching an efficient-looking crime scene investigator busily dusting for fingerprints. The name tag on her shirt read CSI Tina Fowler. I said hello to the freckle-faced lady when she was close to me. She smiled and said she was sorry for my loss and kept working.

"Do you mind if I ask you a couple of questions?"

CSI Fowler looked around and then back at me before saying, "Okay."

I had watched so much crime TV that I already had an idea of what questions I wanted to ask her. She stopped what she was doing and gave me her undivided attention.

"What was the time of death?"

"That hasn't been determined yet, but we will

have an answer soon," she said. "I can assure you that we will find out how your parents were killed. The medical examiner will determine if these were homicides, accidents, or natural deaths . . ."

"Natural?" I asked, cutting her off. "Come on, did that look natural to you?"

"It's the medical examiner's job to determine these things," the lady said. "If it was foul play, we'll get the culprits."

After hours of going through our place and taking down all of our information, the cops were finally gone. I was still comforting my brother when my uncle came out of our rooms with two bags of clothes. We were going to live with him. We left that apartment that morning and never looked back. The case of my parents went unsolved due to the lack of evidence, because the toxicology reports came back inconclusive, and no suspects. I had gotten away with murdering my parents. My mom didn't deserve it, but she was guilty by association, because she knew what my father did but did nothing to protect me.

~ ~ ~

The next year was okay for my brother and me. My uncle gave us everything we needed, especially the love that two kids deserved. He made us happy to be there. June 6, that suddenly changed when my uncle and brother were in a fatal accident. They were on their way to pick up my birthday cake from the store when a Mack truck ran a red light and smacked into the driver's side of his car, then exploded. They never had a chance to react and died on the scene.

My whole life had done a 360 and spiraled out of control. I had no one to care for me, so I went into a deep depression, blaming everything on everyone but myself. Once I found out the truck driver's name, I met him at a bar and propositioned him for sex. Who would have known how many predators there were in the world? I was only seventeen, and this fifty-plus-year-old man was agreeing to take me home with him. I think that's what triggered my murdering spree.

We were sitting at a rest stop off of the interstate, in his truck. I didn't want to go to a hotel because there would be too many witnesses.

"So how do you want to do this, honey?" the man asked, touching my leg. He reached for my breast, but I moved back a little.

"Let's get in the back, and I'll show you the best time of your life," I said.

"Oh lordy, girl, don't hurt this poor ol' man," he smirked, stepping back into the cabin part of the truck.

I reached into my bag and pulled out a syringe filled with another deadly substance and held it close to my side. When he reached down to move his bag off the mattress, I stuck him in the ass, inserting the liquid into his bloodstream. He immediately started convulsing, then went into shock. I tried to exit the truck, but he grabbed my arm tightly. I couldn't break free from him, so I started punching him with my free hand. White foam gushed out of his mouth as he collapsed onto the mattress. I unhooked his huge fingers from my wrist, removed the money from his pockets, then used one of his jackets to wipe everything I touched.

"That's for my little brother," I spat, then stepped out of the truck.

I went inside the rest stop to use the bathroom. After making sure I looked the part, I called an Uber. While waiting, I got something to eat until it came. I had some decisions to make because I was really on my own now with no one to take care of me.

RING! RING! RING!

The sound of the phone broke me out of my daydream. I had been dreaming about my terrible past for the last few weeks, but it wasn't in so much depth as it was now. The newspaper of my latest victim was spread out across the table. The police said they had arrested the wrong person. Why would they do that publicly though? They could have had the upper hand in trapping me, but now I know. Were they intentionally trying to tip me off to see if I would try to make a run for it? They must have thought I was stupid or something. I'd show them exactly what I was capable of. They would never catch me unless I wanted them to.

RING! RING! RING!

It was my job. I already knew what they wanted, I just didn't feel like talking to them right now. I hadn't even had my cup of coffee yet.

"Hello!"

"Get your ass here now. Something has come up, and we need all hands on deck."

"I'll be there soon," I replied.

"Don't be long, and I'm getting sick of you thinking you can just come to work when you want. This is a business, and if you can't abide by the rules, then maybe you should start looking elsewhere."

"I said I'm on my way," I snapped back, then ended the call before they had a chance to respond. "Maybe you will be my next victim," I mumbled to myself, heading back into my bedroom to get ready. "That sounds so good to me!"

CHAPTER TWO

"**SO WHAT HAVE WE** learned so far?" Eric asked, sitting at his desk.

"Well this wasn't some random shit," Sonya began. "Eric, his whole family was executed, and they didn't even spare his kids. Whoever this person is, they have no heart, nor feel sympathy for anyone. If he can do that to them, what do you think he will do to us when we come after him?"

"Hopefully we'll get the chance to find out and bring him, or her, in peacefully."

The two detectives started going over the case again, piece by piece, looking for anything they may have overlooked the first time. Sonya's thoughts were on something totally different from work though. She was still thinking about that night with her partner. She knew he was a player, but she needed him, wanted him, craved him right now. She continued staring at him, tapping her pencil against the side of her face until he looked up and smiled.

"You alright partner?" he asked, sitting the folder down and leaning back in his chair.

"Yeah, why you ask me that?"

"Because you look like you're in deep thought about something. Care to share?" She looked at him for a minute, contemplating if she should just come out and say how she felt or not. Eric gave her this smile that made her panties moisten. "You find anything?"

"No, not yet. I was just thinking about how we got this wrong," she replied, changing the subject.

"Did they let her go yet?"

"Yes, the boss made us release her as soon as we found out about the recent homicides. He figured, how could she have done that from here?"

"It could have been a copycat or something."

"No, this was well planned, Eric. Besides that, he's convinced that no woman could have done this without some massive help. Maybe we did jump the gun on this. Brass was looking to close this as quickly as possible, and we gave them the wrong person."

"So let's do what we do best and make it right. We can start by going out to the crime scene. Hopefully there's something that can help us put this puzzle together."

"I put a couple of plainclothes units on her, just in case she's really not so innocent."

"That's a good idea. That's why you're such a wonderful detective, Sonya," Eric smirked. She playfully punched him in the arm. "Ouch, you know that's my spot."

"Whatever. We have to stop by my place real quick so I can change clothes. Plus, I need you to help me lift something if you don't mind."

"No problem. Let's go," Eric said, holstering his weapon and tucking his phone inside his jacket.

Sonya smiled to herself, knowing the real reason she needed to change clothes. She had been so turned on that pre-cum had leaked out all over her panties and seeped through her khakis.

~ ~ ~

Eric sat down on the couch while Sonya went into the bedroom to change clothes. He was looking around at how clean her place was. He could tell that she barely used it because there wasn't hardly any trash in the trashcan and everything was spotless.

"Damn, you need to come over to my place and clean it for me," he joked.

"In your dreams," Sonya shouted. "You must be gonna pay me to be your maid."

"What did you need me to lift while I'm waiting for you?"

"This," she said, standing in the doorway. When Eric turned around, Sonya was wearing a tightly fitted red nightgown and a pair of heels. His eyes lit up with excitement. "I need you to help me lift this over my head because it's too tight."

"What are you doing? We have a crime scene that we need to get to." Sonya slowly walked over to where he was sitting. "We don't have time for this right now."

"Chill, partner. We have nothing but time. Believe me, that crime scene ain't going anywhere," she said, sitting on his lap.

That was all it took for Eric to have a change

of heart and settle down. She could feel his package through the pants he was wearing. He wrapped his arms around Sonya and kissed her neck. She reached down and put her hand around his bulge, then started kissing him. Sonya began rubbing her hands over his muscular arms. Eric squeezed her ass, feeling the softness between his fingers. She rubbed his bald head as he pulled her back toward his lips and gave her an exquisite kiss.

"I knew you wanted me just as much as I've been wanting you," Sonya moaned.

"I did," Eric said. "I do."

Sonya started playing with his buttons and his belt loops, lifting up her leg and pulling back her nightgown so he could see the vacant place where her underwear had once occupied. She touched her shaved lips and stroked one finger on her pussy, and then traced it across his upper lip.

"Smell me," Sonya said. Eric inhaled deeply, then reached out to pull her back toward him.

Sonya pulled away and kneeled down so she was between his legs. She pulled his belt out of its latch and started undoing the buttons of his pants. His enormous dick fell free from its captor.

"He's all ready for you." Eric smiled.

Sonya licked the massive head, then took his dick into her mouth. She kept gagging from trying to deep throat the whole thing. She wanted it all down her throat, touching her tonsils. Choking on it, gagging even more, she continued to please him. She could hear moans coming from his mouth, which made her go extra hard.

"Now you can ride me," he said timidly.

"I'd love to ride this monster." Sonya got on top of him and slid her pussy down on his shaft. The head went in, and then she let her weight down so his dick was unilaterally inclined to fuck. "Oh God, you feel so fucking good, baby."

"Yes, ride this dick, girl." Eric wrapped both hands around her, kissing her earlobes and her hair. "It feels too good to stop now."

Eric's fingers started pulling up her nightgown until he had it at her shoulders. He grabbed her titties and held her by them, so she squeezed against his chest. Sonya rocked back on his dick. Then cleverly, Eric moved his body back and forth.

"Just ride me, baby," he said, feeling his balls tightening up.

Sonya took that as her time to show him that it was him she had been longing for. She arched her back and let his dick plop out of her, then let it slide right back in, filling her hole with pleasure. As he was holding her waist with one hand, Eric's other hand was sliding down her soft bare skin and reaching for her clit. He licked his middle finger and started circling it, until he made her cum.

"Oh shit," Sonya moaned.

"Don't move," he said as she was gasping from how sweet his fingers felt. She tried, but couldn't help herself because his fingers and dick were feeling too good to her. She was grinding her pussy down on him and looking at him so she could see his grinning face. Within minutes, the two of them were both cumming in unison, Sonya for the second time.

"So I guess we should go try to catch us a

killer now before we both get fired," Eric smirked, standing up to fix his clothes.

"Yes, I guess you're right. Let me take a quick shower and I'll be ready," Sonya replied, heading toward the bathroom. She turned around and faced him as her gown slid from her body and hit the floor. "Care to join me?"

"Naw, I want your scent to marinate on me so I can have something to look forward to later. I can stay here with you tonight, right?"

That must have been what Sonya wanted to hear because she formed the biggest smile she ever made on her face before saying, "Sure, I don't see why not." She walked into the bathroom, leaving the door open just in case he changed his mind. Eric poured himself a drink, then made a phone call.

CHAPTER THREE

SNOW WAS BEGINNING TO fall as I slipped into the alleyway. A ruddy-skinned man with a salt-and-pepper beard and unruly hair walked right past me like he didn't see me. He was probably too busy looking for his next hit or something. I was dressed in dark clothes, gloves, and a snap-brim cap with the earflaps down. As I moved deeper into the alley, I knew I was leaving tracks in the snow but didn't care.

Forecasts were calling for six inches before dawn, and I planned to be finished and gone long before the storm ended. I walked all the way to the rear gate of a beautiful old brick house that was located at the end of the alley. After a long, slow look around, I climbed the gate and crossed a small terrace to a door I'd picked earlier in the evening after bypassing the alarm system. It was six thirty in the morning. I had half an hour at most for what I was going to do.

I shut the door quietly behind me. I stood a moment, listening intently. Hearing nothing to disturb me, I brushed off the snow while waiting for my eyes to adjust to the darkness. Once I could see, I put blue surgical booties over my boots and walked down the hallway to the kitchen. I pushed the chair aside, which made a squeaking noise on the tile floor. It didn't matter because there was no one home. The owners of the house were vacationing out in Miami.

I went to a door on the other side of the kitchen, opened it, and stepped down onto a set of steep wooden stairs. Shutting the door behind me left me in an inky darkness. I closed my eyes and flipped on the light. After waiting again for my vision to adjust, I climbed down the stairs into a small, musty basement piled with boxes and old furniture. I ignored all of it and went to a workbench with tools hanging from a pegboard on the wall.

"Let's get started," I said to myself, shrugging off the knapsack I had on my back.

I removed the leather gloves, and replaced them with latex ones, then unzipped the bag and retrieved four bubble-wrapped packages, which I laid on the bench. I cut off the bubble wrap and stowed the pieces in the pack before turning to admire the Voodoo Innovations Ultra Lite barreled action in 5.56×45mm NATO. My new toy was going to be a work of art.

I fitted the barreled action to a five-ounce minimalist rifle and then screwed a sound suppressor onto the threaded crown of the barrel. Next, I picked up the Zeus 640 optical sight and clipped it neatly into place. Overall, I was pleased with how the gun had turned out. I had ordered the components from a wholesaler online and had them shipped to the same nonexistent person at four separate UPS stores in and around the city of Cleveland.

"This is the perfect tool for this job," I thought, looking through the lens of the scope.

I put the knapsack over my shoulder, took the gun up the basement stairs, and shut the light off before opening the door to the dark kitchen. I stepped out, pushed a button on the side of the sight, and raised the rifle. The Zeus 640 was a thermal unit, which meant it allowed the user to see the world as heat images. When I peered through the scope, the interior of the house looked like it had been cast in pale daylight, except for the heat registers. They showed in much brighter white. The scope had been developed for hog hunters, and it had cost me a lot of money, but it was going to be worth every penny. It was far superior to the kinds of rifle optics any special assault team was using.

I kept the gun pressed snuggly to my shoulder, climbed the stairs to the second floor, and entered the master suite at the front of the house. I ignored all the antique furniture and walked over to the window. Lowering the rifle and opening the window, I saw the branches waving in the background and the silhouette of distinguished townhouses up and down the street.

I raised the gun again and peered through the sight. The snow-covered street and brick sidewalks turned dull black. The heated townhouses, however, were revealed in extraordinary detail, especially the one to my right and down the street. I swung the gun toward the front door of the hot house and studied the area, figuring I'd have four seconds, maybe less when it counted. The brief time frame didn't faze me. I was good at my trade, as you can tell from my previous encounters. I'm sort of used to dealing with short windows of opportunity. You can call me cocky or even confident, but I haven't been caught yet.

I reached into my pocket and pulled out a microchip that I fitted into a slot in the scope in order to record my actions for posterity, then relaxed and waited.

"Patience. This is going to be fun," I mumbled to myself.

Ten minutes later, a light came on in the house to my far diagonal right. I checked my watch. It was 7:00 a.m. on the dot.

"Right on schedule."

Fifteen minutes after that, a black Suburban rolled up the street, also right on time. The wind was blowing stiffly, which told me that I would have to account for a slight bullet drift. The Suburban pulled over by the curb across from the house. I flipped the safety off and settled in, aiming at the front door and the steps down to the sidewalk. The passenger, a large male wearing dark winter clothes, got out of the SUV, ran across the street, and climbed the steps, ringing the bell. The door opened, revealing a woman in a long overcoat.

I couldn't make out her features or determine her age through the thermal scope. Truthfully, I really didn't want to. Through my scope, she was a pale white creature in a cold dark world, waiting to join so many others on the dark side, and I rather liked it that way. As the woman raised her hood and stepped out into the storm, I aimed at the right edge of her head to account for the drift.

"It's showtime," I whispered.

She followed the big guy, hurrying down the stairs, across the street, eager to be out of the snow and get to her early yoga class. Too bad she would never make it. I pulled the trigger, and the rifle made a soft thudding noise. The woman's head jerked back, and she crumbled onto the street behind the man that was walking in front of her.

My first instinct was to flee, but I stayed on task, moving the crosshairs to her chest and shooting her again. I then aimed at the man who thought he had gotten out of my sight, and fired. The bullet went through the car's window and hit him in the neck. I pushed down the sash and never looked back. After finding the missing cases, I rapidly disassembled the gun and placed three of the components back in the knapsack. I kept the thermal scope out and used it so I could move quickly back through the house.

After I slipped out of the rear gate, I turned off the scope and placed it in my pocket. Hearing the wailing of police sirens already, I ducked my head and set off into the storm without being noticed. It felt good starting my killing spree back up again. I never realized how much I had been missing it, but now I was back in the game.

~ ~ ~

Eric and Sonya arrived at the latest crime scene shortly after dawn. It had been a long forty-eight hours for the two detectives, leaving one crime scene to head to another. They had been investigating the Bachman family murder, and it was cold as ice. On their way back to the station, they got a call over the radio to report to a double homicide on Rockside Road. When they pulled up, CPD patrol cars had blocked off both ends of the street. They showed their identification to one of the officers.

He said, "There's Feds and Secret Service

agents already up there."

"I'd imagine so," Sonya said, looking at all the men in black, taking pictures and conversing with each other.

They walked through the barrier and up the street, noticing many anxious residents looking out their windows. FBI criminologists had set up a tent around the victims and the crime scene. Yellow tape was strung from both sides of the townhouse, across the street, and around the Suburban, where a big man in a black parka was engaged in a shouting match with a smaller man in an overcoat and ski cap. Once Eric got closer, he could see that it was his boss arguing with the guy wearing the ski cap.

"This is our case," the chief said. "They died on my goddamn watch."

"The Secret Service will be part of the investigation," the big man in black barked. "But you and your people, Chief Myers, will not interfere with this investigation. You are compromised and will be treated as such."

"Compromised?" Chief Myers said, and for a second, I thought he was going to deck the Agent.

Then FBI special agent Ruben Cezare appeared from behind the tent.

"That's enough," Cezare said. "Agent Pride, please do not assume in any way that you are in charge of this investigation. The FBI has complete jurisdiction."

"Says who?" Agent Pride said.

"Your boss, who should be contacting you right . . . about . . . now," he said, checking his watch. As soon as he finished his statement, the agent's phone rang. He answered it, spoke with the caller for about forty seconds, and then ended the call. Cezare continued, "Evidently, your boss doesn't have much faith in the Secret Service these days. He talked with the director, and the director talked to me, and here we are."

Agent Pride looked furious but managed to keep his voice somewhat under control as he said, "The Secret Service will not be cut out of this."

"The Secret Service will not be cut out. However, it will be put on a short leash and will do what it is told to do," Cezare said. Then he saw Eric and Sonya standing there. "Detectives Lee and Morris, I want you both on this with

Chief Myers."

Quick introductions were made. Secret Service special agent Johnathan Pride had worked Treasury investigations for the past ten years. The big guy was the CPD's chief of police, Ronald Myers. Chief Myers had been working on the victim's security detail for the past couple of weeks because the victim was his high school friend. Between the snow falling and the wind blowing, Myers hadn't heard the fatal shots or the sound of both the woman and man hitting the ground. When he saw them lying on the ground, he immediately sprang into action, calling for backup and hopping out of the car in search of the suspect. Somehow, the shooter had gotten away, and the chief of police was left standing there with two dead bodies on his hands—one who just happens to be a very big politician.

"I was sitting in the car like I always do, when her escort went to hold the umbrella for her as she walked to the car," Myers said. I checked the rearview mirror, making sure no traffic was coming, and when I looked back, they were both lying in the snow bleeding to death. I've been on the force over twenty years. How the hell did I not see that coming?"

"It's not your fault, Chief. That could have happened to any one of us," Eric said.

"That woman was a great person, treated everyone just right."

That was true. The senator from Ohio could be tough when she was fighting for a cause, and she had a first-rate mind, but she was one of those genial and compassionate women. Miss Louise Walker was also the mother of two and a wife.

"Can we see the scene?" Eric asked as the snow slowed to flurries.

Agent Pride said, "Why exactly are you here, Detective Morris?"

"I was about to ask the same thing."

"Because I asked him to be here. I know you're working a very sensitive case right now, but we could really use your expertise on this."

"Okay, we'll try to help any way we can. I guess my boss doesn't have a problem with us working overtime on this."

Pride looked like he'd tasted something disagreeable and threw his hands up in disgust.

FBI Agent Cezare let them look at the crime scene from the flaps of the tent. They went as a pack of five past Chief Myers's Suburban and around the other side of the shelter. Inside, a team of Quantico's finest were working in baggy white jumpsuits pulled over their winter gear. Senator Walker lay twisted on her side in the snow. Her hood was half off her head, revealing a bullet hole beneath her right cheekbone. Her security detail was lying right beside her on his back. Eric knew he wasn't wearing a vest by the bullet that went through his chest.

"What do you know, Kim?"

Kimberly Wilkerson, the chief FBI criminalogist on the scene, stood up from beside the victim. She looked no more than forty-one.

"The snow's making it tougher than tough, Ruben, but so far, it looks like she was hit twice and he was hit once. The headshot killed her instantly. The shooter put a second round into her chest after she fell."

"Overkill, but why?" Sonya stated. "It was like someone was filled with hate."

"Or a professional," Agent Pride said.

"Or both," Eric chimed in. "Who had reason

to hate her if she was so lovable?"

"Good question," Cezare said, and he looked back to Wilkerson. "Got an angle for the shots yet?"

The criminologist made a sour expression. "The snow and no witness to them falling make the first shot tough to call, but by the chest wound, I'm saying it's roughly this angle," she said, gesturing high into the corner of the tent.

Cezare thanked her then turned to Chief Myers. "Is there anything else you can tell us about what you saw when this all happened?"

"Everything happened so fast. I played the scenario over and over again in my head, and I still can't figure out how it happened. The shooter had to be hiding in one of those buildings over there. He got away to quick and easy. I have to get this son of a bitch."

"And we will, but you have to let us do our job," Eric said.

"I have to go break the news to her husband," Chief Myers said, shaking his head.

"Wait," Agent Pride said. "You can't go. You are compromised, and until we clear you, you have to stay with us. It's protocol."

"I'm a well-decorated officer in this city. For you to think that I had anything to do with this is ludicrous and absurd. And another thing, watch your mouth spitting accusations like that. I'm still the chief of police," Myers stated, getting in his face.

"Which means you should understand that I'm doing my job also," Pride said, not backing down.

"How about you go back to locking money launderers up or something?"

"Gentlemen, relax before neither of you are working this case," FBI agent Cezare yelled out. "Chief, I respect that this is your city, but the senator is a federal responsibility, which means we have seniority. I said you and your team can run point for now, but please don't make me call the commissioner to have you taken off of this. As for you, Agent Pride, one more thing from you, and you'll be doing just what he said."

Eric and Sonya stood there listening in awe at how their boss was being talked to. From the look on his face, Eric knew that it was a matter of time before he snapped.

"Excuse me," Eric said. "How about me and

the chief go talk to the husband together, and Sonya can stay here and help Agent Pride?"

"I don't think that's a good idea," Pride intervened.

"He knows the family," Eric said. "Better than any of us. That helps."

"But—"

Eric hardened. "Do you honestly think my chief could be involved with something as heinous as this?"

"Well, no, but it's . . . it's gotta be against protocol," Pride sputtered.

"I don't give a damn about protocol," Eric snapped, surprising everyone, including FBI agent Cezare. "He's in on this investigation, or we walk and let y'all handle it."

"Okay, you go with the chief and talk to her husband. Detective Lee, you don't mind helping Agent Pride, do you?" She nodded her head, then Cezare continued, "Johnathan, take several of your men with y'all, and figure out where the hell those shots came from."

They knocked on the doors of two townhouses across the street that seemed likely candidates and found the residents home and upset. One, a prominent patent attorney, said her next-door neighbors were at their winter home in Miami, and had been for more than two months. Agent Pride quickly got on his phone and called the Robinsons' Florida residence to get permission to enter their home, but got no answer.

When they found snowed-over tracks coming out of the rear terrace and discovered the rear door unlocked and the alarm system bypassed, Johnathan and Sonya felt they had more than enough probable cause to enter. There was water in the hallway, probably melted snow, and smaller droplets crossing the floor to a door to the basement. There was no sign beyond that, certainly not of the footprints they expected to find, given that the shooter came in and out of the weather.

They looked out the front window and decided the shooter had been higher, upstairs. Once they went up the stairs, they found a clear line of sight in the master bedroom, some hundred yards down the street from the evidence tent in front of Senator Walker's house.

"He was right here," Sonya said, looking around. "Probably shot from his knees, using the windowsill as a rest."

As they searched the immediate area, Agent Pride found a piece of paper behind the door. He read the contents, but didn't think anything of it. He was about to throw it back on the floor, when Sonya walked up.

"What's that you found?"

"Here, take a look for yourself. It's probably nothing."

Soon as Detective Lee saw the contents, her eyes got big. "This is definitely our case now," she said, calling her partner.

CHAPTER FOUR

HELEN WAS SITTING AT the bar. She rarely drank, so after one martini, she could feel the effects. The way it made her feel had her ready to start fingering herself right there on the stool. It took the edge off, loosening her tension and sharpening her sensations so that her whole being was ripe and extended in sensuous tentacles, like a cross between a mango and an octopus. She looked around the room at all the men. They seemed like exotic creatures to her, that she wanted, no needed, to touch. This is what happens when you haven't had sex in a while. Not to mention that she was fresh out of a marriage to a basketball player that dumped her and kicked her to the curb.

She looked over at a table where a couple of men were having drinks. There was one guy that looked like he wasn't having such a good time, so she decided he would be the chosen one to put out the fire burning between her legs. He glanced over in her direction, staring like he wanted to say something. He let his gaze rest on her for a minute, then went back to talking to his companions. A few seconds later, his eyes returned to her. Helen popped an olive in her mouth and began sucking on it. No chewing, no swallowing. She held his eyes with hers as she held the olive in her mouth. Then she licked her middle finger. The man staring at her raised his eyebrows a bit and flushed slightly. Cool, but not so cool.

Helen made a big show of getting off the stool. Out of the corner of her eye, she saw him watching lustfully as she approached his table, then lightly touched his shoulder with her still-wet finger as she walked by. There was no eye contact. She left the bar and waited on the street, chewing the olive. She would give him thirty seconds, then it would be his loss and on to the next for her. He stepped out of the bar twenty-five seconds later.

"Your luck almost ran out."

"No, you're about to get lucky if you play your cards right."

Helen smiled and walked around to the side of the building. He followed right behind her as she went down to the end of the alley and stepped inside the hallway to keep warm. She leaned up against the heated wall, feeling the heat through her blouse.

"Take your shirt off," she said.

"Oh, I see. Just—take your shirt off? No, 'Hello,' no, 'What's your name?'" he said, a half smile curving the corners of his mouth. He put his hands flat on her chest, just below her collarbone but above her breasts, and left them there. She could feel the heat of his palms, and it made her nipples harden.

"Okay. Hello. I don't need to know your name. Take your shirt off."

"I'll take my shirt off if you—" he moved his hands down her body and put one hand up her skirt "—if you take off your panties." He hooked a finger under the elastic.

She drew her breath in sharply. He looked at her, eyebrows raised, waiting. She nodded her head, and he pulled her panties down to her ankles. She stepped out of them. Helen helped him unbutton his shirt and pull it off, dropping it on the carpet. She ran her hands all over his chest, feeling how ripped his abs were. It looked like his chest was a washboard waiting for her body to be the dirty clothes.

Helen put her hands on his shoulders and pressed down. He smiled and went down, thinking he knew what she wanted, moving his lips up her inner thigh on his way to her love box, but she had other plans for him. Her pussy lips were singing their swollen siren song. Before he could move his lips to her pussy, she maneuvered herself down and commenced to rubbing her wet labia all over his chest, his pecks, his nipples, and his stomach. Helen was moaning as she slipped and slid on his warm terrain. He was breathing hard, smelling her, holding her ass in his hands, feeling her circular hip motions as she smeared him with her juices.

Helen bent her knees more and stretched her hand down so she could grip his dick. It felt hard and alive through the cotton of his pants. He was moaning now, smelling her erotic scent and rocking against her hand. Then he reached up with both hands and pinched her nipples. That was all it took to put her over the edge. It surprised her, the way it happened so suddenly. Usually it would take longer, especially with her husband. She came in three short waves. She pressed hard into him so her pelvic bone and clit connected with his chest.

As the pulsing became less and the feeling subsided, she hung there, knees still bent, breathing hard as she continued stroking his hard-on through his pants. He stood up and rubbed his knees.

"Ouch," he said. "My knees hurt."

"Ugh," she replied. "You are such a cry baby. Man up!"

"I'll show you a crybaby," he said, releasing his dick from its captor. He bent her over, placing her hands on the wall for support, then rammed his penis in her from behind. "Does this feel like I'm soft?"

Helen moaned so loudly that she thought they would attract attention. He pounded away, feeling her juices covering his shaft as it moved in and out. The feeling was so good that it didn't take long for him to shoot his load inside her. When he pulled out, Helen tugged her skirt down. She gave him a hug and a kiss before walking away.

"That's it?" he called after her, putting his

shirt back on. "Let's go back to my place and finish this."

She turned around and said, "You were good, but not that good. I needed that, so thank you." She opened the door and left as he fixed the rest of his clothes. The door opened back up, and someone came in. He kept fixing his clothes, never turning around to see who it was.

"You changed your mind? Let's go," he said, finally turning around. A gun was pointed at his face. "Whoa, who are you?"

"The grim reaper," the shooter said, pulling the trigger.

His body fell back against the wall, then slid down to the carpeted floor. The blood pouring from his body turned the rug from a cream color to a crimson red. The shooter walked up on him, staring at the golf ball-sized bullet hole, then leaned down and stuffed a piece of paper in his mouth. The killer eased back out of the building undetected, leaving the dead man taking his last breath.

~ ~ ~

Sonya walked up to the closed double doors on the fifth floor of Police Headquarters downtown and knocked on the door.

"Come in," the male voice said.

Sonya opened the door and stepped inside the office of Chief Myers. He was on his cell phone, listening intently and nodding. He motioned for her to take a seat, but there were files all over the place, so she stood there and waited for him to finish.

"I'm hearing you," Chief Myers said in a firm tone. "Loud and clear."

He hung up, reached over, and removed a stack of files from the chair, then motioned for her to sit down. A minute later, Eric came through the door without even knocking, sat some other folders on the floor, and took a seat next to Sonya.

"So where are we on this fucking psychopath?" Myers asked with a serious tone. "And what is this shit I'm hearing about this new case being linked to all our other cases?"

"This was found in a home across the street from where the senator was gunned down," Sonya said, holding up the piece of newspaper that was secured in a plastic evidence bag. "Agent Pride had no idea what he was about to disregard until I asked him to see it. Read what it says."

Sonya removed the clipping and passed it to her partner. Eric unfolded it, and read it out loud so Myers could hear:

An old flame is relit, causing mad commotion and leaving a distasteful feeling in your mouth.

It's time to reveal your true identity.

"What does that mean?"

"I'm not sure, Chief, but I think we will be finding out soon enough," Eric said, reading the horoscope again to himself.

"Some newspapers are calling this bastard the Horoscope Killer because he keeps leaving these signs after a killing," Sonya said, placing the clipping back into the evidence bag.

"Well that was the mayor on the phone again, ringing my fucking head off. It seems like the FBI wants to run point on this because all of them are linked with the senator, and they think we've had this case long enough without solving it," Chief Myers said, tapping his fingers on the desk.

"They can't do that. I thought we already

talked about this," Eric snapped.

"They can, and they will if we don't hurry up and find a prime suspect in the next seventy-two hours. He wants to be briefed every morning so he can decide if it will be out of our hands or not. They still will be running point on the senator's case because of its high profile. I'm not going to give them this whole case though."

"How about we let them think they're running point on the whole thing, but we do our own investigation also without telling them everything?" Sonya suggested.

"Then we would have the resources of the FBI at our disposal, which could be a good thing," Eric chimed in as he looked over a file on the desk.

"Just make sure you are discrete about this. They are already thinking I should be a suspect. I don't need to lose my job too. I'm already getting too much heat from the mayor, commissioner, governor, and even congressmen. They're all wondering how we're not out front on these murders in our own backyard. I'm wondering this too."

CHAPTER FIVE

ELAINE SAT THE PLATE of food down on the table next to the cup of coffee and went to retrieve the toast from the toaster. As she was spreading the butter over it, Tony came down the steps wearing only a towel. He had only been out of prison for a week now and still took more than three showers a day, trying to wash the scent off his body. It had been hell for him.

"Your food is ready," Elaine said, giving him a peck on the lips.

Tony squeezed her ass, pulling her into his embrace. "How about I have you for breakfast? Then afterward, I'll eat the real food." He lifted her up on the counter, spreading her legs and feeling on her pussy through her panties. It was wet.

"That sounds like a plan to me," Elaine replied, placing her arms around him as he kissed her neck. Her cell phone beeped, indicating that she had a text, followed by ringing. "Hold on for a minute. Hello," she said, answering it.

"Turn on the news," the caller said.

"Where are you?"

When the caller told her where she was, Elaine quickly hopped off the counter and grabbed the remote to change the channel. When she turned on the news, she could see what her friend was talking about. The whole time she was talking, Tony was standing in front of her, dick in hand, stroking himself.

"I need you down here with me," the caller said.

"I'm on my way," Elaine said, knowing that it wasn't a request. Even though she was the boss, her team needed her right now. After hanging up the phone, she took another look at Tony's manhood, licked her lips, and shook her head. "I'm gonna have to take a raincheck on that, but I promise to make it up to you when I get home if you're still here."

"You don't have to explain anything to me. Work calls. I'll just watch Pornhub until you get back home." Tony smirked. "Don't forget to change those panties."

"Shut up, boy!"

Elaine gave him a kiss and then went upstairs to her room to get ready. She really had to change her panties because they were soaking wet with pre-cum. A half hour later, she was in her car and on her way to meet up with the rest of her team.

~ ~ ~

Nicole drank from a cup of hot coffee as she surveyed the scene inside the apartment on Otter Avenue. The victim, a white male in his fifties, sat slumped in a chair. Blood had spilled from his neck wound to his lap and clotted on his chest and belly like an apron. The scene wasn't one of the worst she'd seen, but it was a gruesome one. She walked over to where a woman was snapping pictures with a digital camera.

"Time of death?" Nicole asked Evelyn Zverev, the top medical field examiner. She had been called in to replace the old one, who was out on medical leave. She had been in a car accident. There was no timetable of when she would be returning.

"Four or maybe five hours ago?" said Zverev, a tall, lanky woman who used to play basketball at Temple University in Philadelphia. "The heat was turned up, so I'll need more tests to be precise."

"Nasty neck wound. The knife?" Nicole said, gesturing to a switchblade on the carpet near the corpse's body. It looked like it was really sharp.

Zverev shook her head no. "That's his knife. There's a scabbard for it around his right ankle, and there's no sign of blood on the blade."

"So what was the weapon?"

The ME pulled out a pair of reading glasses, then peered at the victim's neck. "He's got bruising and skin abrasions above and below the wound, and the edges are ragged. Could be a thin rope, but I'm thinking some kind of small-gauge wire."

"From behind?"

"I'd say so," Zverev said. "The killer had to be pretty strong for the wire to cut deep like that, and smart. The victim got a shot off with that 9 mm in the corner, but missed their target."

"No one heard the shot?"

Dwight Parks, the other detective on the scene, said, "No one yet."

"We have an ID? Who found him?" asked Nicole.

Detective Parks said they found a driver's license and credit cards that identified the deceased as Darrell Turner of Beechwood, Ohio, and business cards that pegged him as a medical equipment salesman. A maid that worked for the apartment's owners had arrived to bring clean towels around 7:00 p.m. and found Turner unresponsive, in his present state.

"I've already spoken with the owners," Parks said. "Turner booked online nine days ago. He indicated in his application he was going to combine business with pleasure and stay for four nights."

Nicole thought about that. "Anything linking him to the murder a couple of blocks away?" Parks and Zverev both seemed surprised by the question. "Two killings a week apart and five blocks apart? This guy was armed not only with a pistol, but also a knife he carries in an ankle sheath. So until we prove otherwise, we're considering these murders connected. Meanwhile, Detective, I want you to run his prints. Anything else? Itinerary? Phone? Computer?"

Parks shook his head. "Nothing beyond the wallet and IDs. Doesn't this mean we will have to let the FBI, the Secret Service, and the two detectives that are working the senator's murder case know that we have another body?"

"You let me worry about that," Detective Carson stated, pulling out her cell phone to call Sonya. Just as she was scrolling through her phone log, a call broke through. It was dispatch. Nicole sighed and answered. "This better be good. I'm in the middle of another crime scene."

"Detective Carson, we've had officers under fire, a high-speed chase, and now an armed standoff with multiple weapons involved," the dispatcher said. "Detective Lee asked me to contact you and have you meet her there ASAP."

"I was just about to call her. I'm on my way there now," Nicole said to dispatch.

Nicole started toward the door at a fast pace, still barking questions at the person on the phone. She was told that it started when a CPD patrol unit had pulled over a Cadillac Escalade with Ohio plates for failure to make a full stop at a stop sign. There were three males in the car.

The officer ran the plates and found them registered to Miguel Feliciano of Cleveland. The name sounded familiar.

"What do you have on him?" Nicole demanded, leaving the apartment crime scene.

"Miguel's a big-time gangbanger with ties to the Mexican drug cartels. He's got a long history of violence and three felony warrants out for his arrest, including one for threatening bodily harm to an eighty-year-old woman."

"Thanks, I have to go now," Nicole said, ending the call.

~ ~ ~

Nicole arrived on the scene in twenty minutes after she hung up the phone. Patrol cars had blocked off both sides of Slyman's Tavern.

"Anyone called the FBI yet?" she asked a patrol officer.

"Not yet, Detective. Chief Jones called and said Detective Lee will be running point on this though."

"So why did she call me? I could be doing other things right now."

"Because you're her best friend," the officer

replied with a slight grin on his face.

"Well, that is true, isn't it, Officer Elliott?" Nicole said with a smile of her own. She winked her eye at the young officer, then headed in Sonya's direction.

She ducked under the crime scene tape and kept low as she hustled toward another patrol car up the block where Sonya was crouched down with two other officers, with their weapons drawn. The side windows of the cruiser were blown out. So was the windshield. Half a block beyond them, in the middle of the street, there was a midnight-blue Cadillac Escalade with Ohio plates and an abandoned city snowplow.

"Nice of you to join us," Sonya said as Nicole ducked down.

"Yeah, yeah, if you missed me that much, you could have called me for drinks, girl. You know I'm a sucker for a martini."

"You haven't changed one bit."

"I know," Nicole said. She looked at the two officers that were there with her. "You're the ones who pulled them over?"

"Kronwall and Collins, ma'am," said officer Kronwall, a blonde in her thirties. She told Nicole the same thing she told Sonya, that getting the alert regarding Feliciano's felonies had taken long enough to make the gangbanger and his friends anxious. "When they saw me climb out of the car, one of the two in the back opened fire, and Feliciano hit the gas.

"They gave chase for more than a mile before Feliciano saw the snowplow coming at them. They couldn't get around the plow, and they abandoned the Escalade in the middle of the street. Armed with pistols and AR-style rifles, Feliciano shot at the snowplow, shattering the windshield and sending the operator scrambling out the other door and down the street. One of the other two opened up on the patrol car before the three of them forced their way into a yellow Craftsman bungalow on the north side of the street."

"Time of last shots?"

"Nine minutes ago," Collins said. "And we've got officers watching the back of the house. They're still in there."

"Hostages?"

"We're assuming so," Sonya said. "According to city records, residents are Mathew Sheridan, his wife, Sienna, and their eight-year-old twins, Emma and Kate."

Before Nicole could respond, a gun went off in the house. A woman started screaming, and then girls' shrill voices joined her. Sonya radioed dispatch, reported the shot and the hostages, and requested that the entire neighborhood be cordoned off. Sonya clicked off, and her phone immediately rang. It was Eric.

"What's happening, partner?" he asked.

She told him everything she had learned about the shooters since arriving on the scene, and Nicole was there as her backup.

"If you need me, I'm only a phone call away."

"We got this, but thanks," Sonya said, ending the call. At the same time, Nicole had received a call from the chief.

"What's happening?" he demanded.

"When pulled over for a traffic stop, he and his men responded with violence, and they've taken hostages in the process. There's also a homicide victim on Otter Avenue, who may or may not be involved."

"Jesus," Carol said. "What do y'all need from me?"

She looked down the street behind her and saw a big black SWAT van pulling up. She exhaled a bit knowing that the answer to that question had just been answered.

"The calvary just arrived, Chief," Nicole said. "I'll let you know if anything—" More screams came from the house. "Sorry, Chief, gotta go."

She hung up and peeked over the hood of the patrol car. Sonya was already looking. Emma and Kate, the terrified twins, came out the front door, followed by two gangsters. The men were wearing kerchiefs over their lower faces, holding on to the collars of the sisters' nightgowns and pressing pistol muzzles to the backs of the girls' heads, using the children as human shields.

"We ain't waiting for no SWAT or negotiators," one shouted. "Get that plow the hell out of here. You let us move, or we kill them and go out in a blaze!"

"No!" a woman screamed.

Sonya peeked again and saw a brunette in a Cleveland Browns jersey, jeans, and socks come out the door with the third man behind her. Sonya recognized Feliciano from the picture dispatch had sent. He held an AK-47 pressed to the back of the sobbing woman's head. He said something to her.

"Believe him!" she cried. "He shot my husband. He'll kill us all."

"So what's it gonna be?" Feliciano yelled as his men started down the front steps. " A peaceful ending? Or a goddamned bloodbath?"

Nicole took the bullhorn the officer had pulled out and looked at Sonya for confirmation. Sonya nodded.

"This is detective Nicole Carson of the Ohio State Police Department," she said, trying to sound calm. "No one wants bloodshed here, Mr. Feliciano."

"Then let us leave!" Miguel yelled. "Now."

"You're going to give me a little time to clear the streets," she called out. "It's not like I have the keys to that snowplow at my fingertips."

"Five minutes, then!" Miguel said.

"Fifteen."

"No. Ten! And after that we don't give a damn about nothing else, and the little girls and mommy gonna start dying, just like that bitch-ass Senator Walker did."

"Did he just say Senator Walker?" Sonya said as he dragged the girls and their mother back inside the bungalow. "I think we have our killer, Nikki." She dropped behind the cruiser and keyed her radio mike. "CPD SWAT, this is Detective Lee."

By this time, there were at least six TV and radio stations on the scene. Sarah and Elaine were two of the reporters. Sarah was looking around for Eric, hoping he was there so she could get an exclusive from him, but he was nowhere to be found. She continued searching the area, when she stumbled across his partner barking orders on a radio. They weren't letting them anywhere near the scene, so she got as close as she could without crossing the barricade and snapped a few pictures.

"Lieutenant Bencic here, Detective. SWAT is armed and ready to deploy."

A plan formulated quickly in her head. "Lieutenant, I need a team ready to push forward in support of my location. I need quality shooters up high, with a clear view of that Land Rover, and put teams on porches on the southwest and northwest corners of the block.

Your best officers. Block off all the surrounding areas."

"Roger that!"

"Seven minutes, Lee," Miguel yelled from the house.

"I hear you, Mr. Feliciano," she said through the bullhorn. "We're trying to find the snowplow operator. We just need a little more time and everyone can get what they want, okay?"

A rattle of gunfire went off inside the house, before he shouted, "There's no trying! We're about doing here, right?"

"Right, Miguel," she said, and then she ducked back behind the cruiser, still working out her strategy. She looked at Nicole. "Where is the snowplow driver?"

"Standing over there with the two officers."

Sonya checked her watch as she ran in that direction. They had six minutes to pull this off. Near the corner, she cut right into an alley that was paralleling the hostage scene. She checked her watch again. Down to five minutes. Sonya hoped she had enough time. Thinking about if it was her kids, Sonya went from a run to a sprint, dodging trashcans and the odd stack of boxes, trying not to slip in the snow. She raced over to the other cruiser that was blocking off the street.

Lieutenant Bencic, strapped in body armor, stood there waiting with two uniformed officers and their cruiser blocking the street. Gasping, she laid out her plan to the SWAT commander. Bencic listened, thought, and then smiled.

"I can do that, Detective, but it's going to cost you big. Bigger than anything you can think of."

"Good," she said, and nodded to the other officers. She also called Nicole to let her know the plan, so she would be ready when the shit hit the fan.

Ninety seconds later, Lieutenant Bencic ran crouched along the snow-packed sidewalk, sticking to the shadows until he was half a block from the snowplow. Sonya watched him through binoculars from the front porch of a townhouse at the southeast corner. Four SWAT officers awaited her command behind her. Another four waited on a porch across the street. The last of the twelve was diagonally across from her on the northwest corner of the intersection with Nicole. Sonya keyed the bullhorn.

"Mr. Feliciano, we are moving the snowplow.

I am assuring you safe passage as long as you leave the hostages behind."

"You think I'm stupid?" he bellowed.

"No, but that's part of the deal," Sonya replied.

"They're staying with us until we decide to let them go. Just move the damn snowplow and get the hell out of our way!"

"Suit yourself," Sonya mumbled as she watched Bencic creep between two cars and angle onto the street itself, keeping the snowplow between him and the Sheridans' bungalow. He then climbed in the open side door. Sonya spoke on the radio. "Nice and easy now, Lieutenant."

"Roger that. I got this."

The snowplow engine turned over. Sonya swung her binoculars to the front porch of the Sheridans' house and saw Mrs. Sheridan and her daughters coming out. Feliciano and his two masked men were behind them.

"Move that goddamned plow!" Miguel shouted.

Bencic lifted the snowplow's blade, turned on the headlights, and drove. Sonya, Nicole, and the rest of the SWAT team watched Feliciano and his men hustling the family off the porch and down the short path toward the sidewalk. The moving snowplow blocked Sonya's view for several moments before Bencic drove past her, slowed, swung the plow in reverse, and backed it up the street heading north.

He stopped the plow about fifty yards from the intersection, right where Sonya wanted him. The plow headlights died. Sonya looked back at the Escalade and saw Miguel already in the front passenger seat aiming his weapon at a trembling Sienna, who was behind the wheel. The other four were in the backseat, one girl at each window, Feliciano's men in the middle.

Calling their positions into her radio, Sonya watched the headlights on the Escalade go on, and the big SUV started toward her.

"Here we go," she said. "On my call, Lieutenant."

"Roger, Detective. Ready!"

Nicole and the SWAT officers ducked low. Sonya pushed back into the shadows, watching through binoculars. For a moment, she held her breath as the Escalade approached the corner. She feared Miguel might turn onto the side street, but he kept coming.

"He's taking the easy way out," Nicole said into her mic.

"I know. Ten seconds, Lieutenant."

The Cadillac's headlights swayed closer. Sonya dropped the binoculars, let them hang around her neck, and drew her service weapon. The snowplow's lights were still off, but Bencic had it moving in a slow roll toward the end of the block. She glanced from the accelerating SUV to the plow and yelled over the radio.

"Now."

She heard the plow's big diesel engine roar and saw it barreling toward the approaching Cadillac. The Escalade almost got through the intersection, but then the forward edge of the plow blade clipped the SUV's right rear quarter and tore off the bumper. On the slick winter surface, the Cadillac was hurled into a sharp, clockwise spin. It smashed into two parked cars. Bencic skidded the plow to a stop, blocking their retreat but not her view.

"Take Feliciano," Sonya said.

A rifle was shot from the rooftop diagonally across the intersection from her, shattering the passenger side of the Cadillac's windshield. The three SWAT teams, led by detective Nicole Carson, exploded from their positions and charged the Escalade. Sonya could see one of the girls screaming in the backseat of the SUV and feared the two other gunmen would execute them before the SWAT teams could set them free. Miguel opened fire with the AK-47 through the Escalade's passenger-side window, blowing it out and hitting two of the SWAT men. They sprawled on the sidewalk behind parked cars. Nicole dove to the ground, catching a bullet to her right shoulder.

"Officers down," she yelled over the radio, switching her weapon from the right to the left side. "I've been hit also."

"Hold on!"

Three SWAT officers opened fire. All three hit one of the bangers, and he crumbled. Blood haloed around him on the snowy street. Lieutenant Bencic pushed open the plow door and leaped down, gun up and aiming through the Escalade's side rear window.

The silhouette of one of Miguel's men was sagged over on one of the twins, who was shrieking in fear. The other gunman had her sister around the neck, a pistol pressed to her head.

"Don't do it! Show me your hands," Nicole shouted. When the suspect didn't move, she said, "Let me put it in a language that you'll understand. Make another move, and my gun goes boom."

The third gunman hesitated and then dropped the pistol. Nicole yanked open the passenger rear door and pulled the sobbing girl out. Bencic ran forward, calling into his radio for the rest of his team to raid the Sheridans' home. Other officers were helping Sienna and her other daughter from the car. Inside the car, the third of Miguel's crew stared straight ahead. Even with the wool hat she wore down over her eyebrows, there was no mistaking her gender. Latina, mid-twenties, she had tattoos of teardrops on her lower cheeks.

There was blood all over her from the dead man beside her. There was a gaping wound in his throat from the SWAT sniper's shot, the one that missed Miguel.

"Hands behind your head," Nicole said. "Fingers laced, and slide to me."

She did. Nicole spun her around and slapped the cuffs on her wrists. She keyed her radio and told dispatch that the hostages were safe, one suspect was in custody, and they needed an ambulance. She didn't bother listening to dispatch's reply but ran past Miguel's corpse to check on the injured officers that were hit in that flurry of gunfire. Sonya was already there helping one of them. Both men had taken rounds that entered their bulletproof vests. They were shaken but alive.

CHAPTER SIX

AROUND SEVEN THIRTY, I watched as my two foster sisters were ferrying plates of steaming scrambled eggs, maple-smoked bacon, and hash brown potatoes with hot sauce.

"You're sure you won't have some?" my foster mother asked Bree, who had walked in the door only twenty minutes before. "I'm going back to bed after y'all leave for school."

"A glass of orange juice would be good," Bree said, stealing a piece of bacon from my plate.

After giving Bree some juice, my foster mom walked into the living room and sat next to her boyfriend, who couldn't keep his eyes off of me. Ever since I came here after my parents were murdered, he would look at me strangely. It would creep me out at times. He was around twenty-eight, and my foster mom was about to turn forty in a week. He looked like one of those basketball players that didn't get a chance to get that big break, so now he was stuck leaching off of a woman that took in kids off of the street for money.

At the age of thirteen, Kensi's mother gave her up for adoption to pursue her drug addiction. She was so strung out on dope that she would leave her own daughter with anyone who would take her. One day she tried to sell her to a neighborhood drug dealer for a couple of bundles. The dealer paid her the dope and took a scared Kensi to his apartment. She thought he was going to rape and kill her when she saw all the other men in the apartment, but he did the opposite. The dealer called Child Services, and they immediately came and placed Kensi in foster care.

Jannie had become an orphan at the age of nine. Both of her parents were killed in a car accident when they were on their way home from having dinner. Her father ignored the signs and blinking lights and tried to cross the tracks, when their car was smacked by an oncoming train. Jannie was home with the babysitter at the time.

Because the babysitter wasn't capable of

caring for Jannie full time, she had to be placed in foster care also. Sherry took the kids in with no problem. They loved her like she was their real mother. There was nothing she wouldn't do for them.

I came about a year later. There was one problem: she could only take one more child, and that child was me. My brother was sent to another family against his will, and there was nothing I could do about it. I tried not to let them take him, but it was out of my control. That left me feeling empty inside for a while. Me and my sisters got along really well with Sherry. My foster father, though, was a different story. He was a piece of shit. The constant looking creeped me out. He never stared at my other sisters the way he stared at me. I guess it was because they weren't as beautiful as I was.

Anyway, one day he took us all to the YMCA so we could go swimming. While we were in the pool, he kept splashing us with water, well, mostly me. I was just trying to enjoy myself, when I felt a pair of hands grabbing me from behind. I turned around and saw that it was him.

He had pulled me so close to him that I could feel his pee-pee on my butt. That suddenly gave me flashbacks to what my biological father used to do to me before I killed him. When I tried to free myself, he tightened his grip and whispered in my ear.

"Stop fighting it. I seen the way you be looking at me when we're home. I like you too!" His hand started moving down my body.

Before he could get anywhere near my vagina, I broke free from him and got out of the pool. Sherry gave me a strange look when I ran to her crying.

"He tried to touch me in the pool," I screamed, causing people to look at us.

"Who?" Sherry said, jumping out of the chair.

"He did," I said.

Sherry snapped out, calling him all kinds of perverts and molesters. He jumped out of the pool and ran out of the building in just his shorts.

"Are you okay?" Sherry asked as everyone staring suddenly went back to doing what they were doing.

"Yes, I just want to go home," I told her.

We all gathered our stuff and went home. My foster father didn't come home until late that evening, and he was drunk. As soon as he walked through the door, he and my foster mother began arguing. It got so heated that he smacked Sherry in the face. Me and my sisters watched from the top of the stairs. They were crying, but I was furious. He would not get away with putting his hands on my mother.

~ ~ ~

Later that night, when everyone was asleep, I snuck out of the house. I walked down the four blocks alone, making sure no one saw me. I was on a mission, and if I was seen, that would defeat the purpose of what I had planned. When I reached my destination, I gently tapped on the door. A minute later, he answered wearing a pair of sweatpants and a wifebeater.

"Why are you here at three in the morning dressed like that?" I was wearing a pair of skimpy shorts and a T-shirt. "You look like a little whore."

"I just came to say that I'm sorry for causing so much trouble." I could tell that he was still drunk and horny by the way his eyes were glued to my tight shirt. "Can I come in, please?"

He looked around, making sure I wasn't trying to set him up, then stood to the side and let me in. There were beer cans lying on the floor, and clothes were scattered all over the couch. To say that his house was dirty would be an understatement. It looked like a hurricane had run through it. I pulled my shorts down to my ankles and stepped out of them. I brushed all the clothes onto the floor.

"Sit down, I have a surprise for you."

"Oh yeah! What would that be?" he said, licking his lips. "You finally going to let me get a taste of that little pussy, huh?"

"I'll let you taste it, after I taste you first."

"Okay!"

He removed his sweatpants and sat on the couch. I did a sensual dance as I made my way over toward him. His eyes were so glued to my body that he never saw me pull out the switchblade that was hidden behind my back. I got down on my knees, in between his legs, and removed his penis from his boxers. He closed his eyes and rested his head back on the couch as I stroked him until he was fully erect. I felt like I was going to throw up at the sight of his uncircumcised penis.

"You ready, Daddy?" I said in a low voice. He opened his eyes so he could watch.

"Go ahead, suck it, baby."

"Yes, daddy. Close your eyes back."

As soon as his eyes were closed, I struck. With one hand gripping his penis, I raised my other one in the air, and in a swift motion, I swung the blade hard as I could. It sliced through like a piece of salami. His eyes popped open, and he screamed out in pain. At the same time, he punched me so hard that I flew backward and hit my head on the table that was in the middle of the floor.

"Ahhhhh, you biiiiitch. I'll kill you," he screamed, trying to hold his severed penis in place.

The back of my head was in so much pain that it felt like I was seeing stars. However, somehow I managed to stumble to my feet and grab the aluminum baseball bat that was lying by the door. I smacked him across the face with it as hard as I could, sending him to the floor. He balled up in a fetal position, trying to cover his face, but I was relentless. Blood was squirting everywhere as I continued to hit him blow after blow.

"You pervert," I said, stumping him in the face.

He passed out on the floor after succumbing to the pain. I picked up the knife, walked over to where he was lying, and inserted it into his jugular artery to make sure he would not get up. He died in a matter of seconds. Not done with him, I carved the words "I'm a pervert" on his chest so when they found his body, they would know what he was.

After I finished what I came there for, I went into the bathroom and washed his blood off of my body. I put my shorts back on and wiped down everything that I touched, leaving the bat and knife there. I didn't care if they found the murder weapons. I was pumped that I was starting to get good at this killing shit. I guess you could blame it on always watching *CSI*,

NCIS, and *Law and Order*. They were my favorite shows.

I snuck out of his house making sure I wasn't seen, just like I did when I first left. When I got back to my house, everyone was still asleep. I lay back in bed like nothing ever happened. The next morning, when we woke up, Sherry was in her room crying. Me and Kensi walked in and sat on the bed next to her.

"What's wrong, Mommy?" Kensi asked.

"Look," was all she said, pointing at the television.

In clear view was my foster father's picture. They said he had been brutally murdered in his home in the middle of the night. The reporter asked that if anyone had any information about what had happened, to contact the CPD. Sherry's crying made me mad, because I thought she was mourning some nigga that liked touching little girls, but come to find out, she was crying because she was happy he was dead.

KNOCK! KNOCK! KNOCK!

Sherry got up to answer the door. When she opened it, two police officers in uniform and one detective were standing there. He flashed his badge before speaking.

"We have a warrant for your arrest."

The two officers cuffed Sherry and pulled her out of the house.

"Noooooo!"

I woke up from my sleep sweating profusely again. I had had another nightmare. They had been coming randomly lately, and I just couldn't shake them. My nightgown was drenched with perspiration. I sat up in my bed and thought about who I would be going after now. Eventually, I knew I would have to prepare for the inevitable, but in the meantime, I was going to take out as many people as I possibly could.

CHAPTER SEVEN

HANDCUFFED AND WEARING AN orange prisoner jumpsuit, the only surviving member of Feliciano's crew glared at the tabletop as FBI agent Ruben Cezare followed detective Sonya Lee into an interrogation room at the federal detention facility. Eric was in an observation booth with US Secret Service agent Johnathan Pride, chief Carol Jones from the Special Investigative Division, and detective Nicole Carson. Nicole only tagged along because they had all agreed this would be a joint operation. The Feds had jurisdiction over the case because the senator was killed, which was the reason she was in federal prison instead of a county one.

"She's asked for an attorney," Eric said.

"Course she did," Chief Jones said bitterly.

Cezare and Sonya took seats opposite her. She raised her head, saw Sonya, and acted as if she'd sniffed something foul. She had spiderweb tattoos on both hands and another climbing the left side of her neck.

"Your prints came up," Cezare said, sliding a piece of paper in front of her. "Lupe Morales. Multiple arrests as a juvenile, four as an adult for soliciting, drug dealing twice, and abetting an armed robbery. Looks like you did three years in prison for that one."

"Eighteen months," Lupe said. Then she yawned. "I've asked for a lawyer. Twice now. So why are you still trying to talk to me?"

"The federal defender's office has been notified," Cezare said. "In the meantime, you can do yourself a whole lot of good by talking to us."

She sniffed. "I've heard that one before."

"The US attorney is preparing to charge you with four counts of kidnapping, two counts of murder, three counts of attempted murder, and two counts of firing on police officers in the course of duty," Sonya said. "Oh, and co-conspirator in the plot to murder a US senator. I'm thinking life without parole times two, for now."

"If not the federal death penalty," Cezare said. "The new administration's big on taking that road whenever possible. Haven't you heard?"

Lupe sat forward, her upper lip curled. "I'm guilty of nothing but being stupid and going along for a ride I should never have been on, know what I'm saying? You can try all you want to twist my words up, but it's not going to work, you understand?"

"No, actually, I don't," Sonya said. "I don't understand a lot of shit. Like, what reason would you have to kill someone?"

"Check my gun," she replied. "That little Glock? No bullets, and not because I ran out. It's clean because I've never fired it. I didn't shoot at no one. Never have. Never will, and especially no fucking senator."

In the booth, Eric put a call in to the FBI lab at Quantico and asked a tech to check her assertion about her gun. He put him on hold. As he waited for an answer, Eric heard Lupe denying knowing exactly why Miguel Feliciano had decided to do what he did, and continuously denied her involvement.

"Only thing I knew is he said he was gonna set some things straight and make a pile of money doing it," Lupe said. "I was just along for the ride."

"Armed to the teeth?" Sonya asked.

"Not me. Like I said, that piece was all for show."

"Tell us about Senator Walker," Cezare said.

"Miguel hated her because she wanted to send his family back to El Salvador. If it wasn't for having that crazy-ass president in office, nobody would be scared of being deported."

"Did he hate her enough to kill her?" Sonya said, writing something down on her notepad.

Lupe thought about that for a moment and then nodded her head. "But he'd have to have been seriously messed up on dope and have her, like, show up at the door when he was all hating the world and shit."

"C'mon, Ms. Morales," Cezare said. "Miguel or his other men or you shot the senator early yesterday from an empty townhouse down the street."

"The hell I did," Lupe said, sitting up, indignant. "Miguel didn't either, or Calvin. We might've hated that bitch, but we sure didn't kill her."

"Miguel confessed," Sonya said. "I heard him. So did two other officers."

"No way!"

"Yes way," Sonya replied sarcastically. "When you were out on the porch with the girls, Miguel and I were negotiating for a few minutes, and he told me we had ten minutes, and after that, he didn't give a damn that the little girls and their mom were going to die just like that bitch senator did."

"So?" Lupe said. "That's no confession. He was just like, comparing it or something."

"That's not the way I heard it."

"You hear it any way you want, that don't make it so. Was Miguel happy she was dead? Totally. He went out into the fucking snow and did a dance when he heard. He even hoped someone took the president out with her, but he did not kill her or her security. None of us did. When she was shot, we were stuck in a shit-hole motel because of that ice storm. You can go check if you want to. I'm sure we're on one of their security cameras there. People can't be in two places at one time. Can they?"

"You let me be the judge of that. We will

check out your alibi, and if what you're saying is true, then you won't have to worry about her death, at least. But, again, if you weren't here to kill the senator, why were you, Miguel, and this Calvin guy in this area in the first place?" Cezare said.

"And armed to the teeth," Sonya added.

"Like I said, I don't know for sure," Lupe said evasively. "I came along for the ride, mostly. I don't really have to answer your questions, but here I am, doing exactly what my lawyer would tell me not to. I have family that lives a block from where all that shit happened, so I guess you can say I had a reason to be there."

"But Mr. Feliciano came there for other reasons," Sonya said. "Maybe to make a lot of money performing a hit. Is that correct?"

"That's what I'm saying."

"Were you going to make money?"

Lupe didn't reply for several minutes. She was contemplating if she should or shouldn't answer the question. "I dunno, maybe. It hadn't been decided if I was in or out yet, or if I was needed."

"To do what?" Cezare asked.

"If I tell you this, will you help me by speaking to the prosecutors?" Sonya looked at Cezare, then back to Lupe, and nodded her head. "They wanted to see if I had what it took to be a drug-and-gun smuggler. Those guns that were in the Escalade were on their way to be sold to some big-time dealers in Beechwood. We were supposed to pick up some money and meet up with the connect later. Before we got there, those cops pulled us over for no fucking reason. Miguel got scared and thought they would try to deport us, so he decided to go out in a blaze of glory. He'd rather be carried by six than be judged by twelve. Anyway, if I would have passed that test, I would've been able to make solo runs for them."

"Who is them?" Sonya asked.

"I never got the chance to meet them. Look, I told you everything I know. That's all I have for you. Are you going to keep your word and help me out of this?"

"That depends. I feel like you're holding something back, and until you tell us everything we need to know, you won't be getting anything from us."

"That's bullshit," Lupe snapped. "You're a piece of shit. If I wasn't in these cuffs, I would—"

There was a sharp knock at the door. A tall, willowy blonde in a fine blue skirt suit and a pearl necklace came in carrying an attaché case.

"Chelsea Taylor, counselor for Ms. Morales," she said crisply. "I'll be representing her from this moment on, and this interview, I'm afraid, is over."

Sonya exited the interrogation room with an agitated look on her face. She was openly angry when she reached the observation booth. Eric was still on hold, waiting for the tech lab to get back to him.

"Feliciano confessed," she said. "Now this fucking lawyer is going to stop us from getting information that I know she was holding back on. I heard it, so did the other officers."

"Lupe says it was just a manner of speaking," Chief Jones said.

"Sure she says that," Sonya replied. "She wants off death row."

"What's Chelsea Taylor doing involved in this case anyway?" Agent Pride said. "She's not with the federal defenders. She's good at high-dollar, white-collar crime cases."

The tech at Quantico came back on the line. Eric listened, thanked him, and hung up. "Morales was right about her gun being empty. In fact, the FBI lab says it's never been fired."

"That doesn't absolve Feliciano of the murder," Sonya said.

"I agree," Nicole said.

"You're both right," Chief Jones stated. "Until we check with that motel, an empty gun doesn't absolve anyone. But you should also know that the ballistics folks at Quantico say that none of the weapons recovered from the crime scene remotely match the bullets that killed Senator Walker, her security, or any of the other murder victims. However, the bullets do match some of the victims', which means, our serial killer has struck again. I think we have to consider the case still active."

CHAPTER EIGHT

TONY WAS AWAKENED BY a knock on the door. He jumped up and was puzzled to find that he was in the bathtub asleep.

"Damn, how long have I been asleep?" he asked himself while wrapping a towel around his waist as he stepped out of the tub. He felt like he'd been asleep for hours, but when he checked his phone, he realized that it had only been twenty-five minutes. "Who is it?"

"Sarah!"

"Who?" he said, and looked out of the peephole before asking himself, "HOW SHE GET PAST SECURITY?"

"Sarah!" she said again, and then he remembered as he studied her face through the peephole.

"Oh shit! Yeah, I remember her now. That's one of Elaine's workers," he said to himself, bewildered as she stood at his door. Tony opened it up, peeked his head out the door, and looked both ways up and down the hallway before stepping to the side and letting her in. "It's cool. Ain't nobody with me or following me. I roll solo," she said bluntly. "I come in peace."

"I heard that," he replied, then asked, "How'd you get up here anyway? I didn't even know you knew where I lived."

"A lil charm, a lil class, mixed with a bit of persuasiveness, and don't forget a whole lot of good looks!" She smiled, speaking the truth. Sarah was very attractive. "She's always talking about you, and when I saw you and her at the restaurant that evening, I made an effort to find out who you were. I dropped her off here one day when her car was getting detailed."

"Damn, that's all it took for you to get past security? I guess we need some better people working the door, huh?" he joked and closed the door. "So what's up? What brings you here?"

"I came over here because we are planning a surprise party for Elaine, and we want to have it here, if that's cool with you," she said with a slight smile on her face, looking around the apartment. "Your place is so nice."

"Thank you! Can I get you something to drink?" he asked, going toward the minibar, which was packed with beverages.

"No, I'm fine." Then there was an awkward moment.

"So you came over here at this time of night to talk about giving Elaine a party?"

"No! That's not all I came for. I just thought you could use a little company, being as though Elaine is so tied up with that high-profile case. Plus, I thought that maybe we need to get to know each other better, since you're messing with my friend and all, feel me?" Sarah said in a deep naughty voice as she switched positions in her seat.

"Do we?" Tony asked.

"Don't we?" she asked matter of factly, batting her eyes and then licking her lips sending a feeling of guilt through his mind. He hadn't even done anything with this woman and already felt like he cheated. He should have never let her in, never opened the door, and now her perfume lingered seductively in the room. The smell was erotic, almost devilish, giving his manhood a semi-erection, and then he remembered he was only wearing a towel.

Sarah saw the print of his dick poking from the towel and got aroused. "LITTLE WHORE!" were the words reverberating through her eardrums as if someone was whispering in her ear, while simultaneously moistening her softness. When he sat down to hide the bulge underneath his towel, she smiled because it only exposed him more. Sarah could see right through the towel, to the thing she loved so much, and his, well, he was blessed. She got excited.

"Why'd you sit down? I already saw it," she teased.

"Saw what?" His embarrassment was evident.

"Your dick. It was getting hard. Must mean, well can only mean one thing," she said and stood up. "One thing," she repeated.

Tony's mouth dropped wide open as Sarah stood up and moved her body like a belly dancer. She was beautiful. She waved her body from side to side like a snake, slowly unzipping her coat, then stopping.

"You like?"

Tony didn't respond. She walked a little closer to him, perfume getting stronger, and placed her hands on his knees as he sat on the edge of the couch. Sarah leaned down, stared him in the face, and watched as he squirmed beneath her power.

"What are you doing?"

"Shhhh, be quiet," she replied, placing a finger over his lips.

Sarah pulled at the towel, but he was sitting on it, so she settled for just opening it up. Tony was still semi-erect, but she was going to change that as she smiled a devilish grin and stepped away from him. She started her belly dance again, but this time letting the coat drop to the floor. She stood stark naked in a pair of high-heel boots that came up to her knees, revealing a set of perfectly shaved legs and thighs. Her pussy lips looked puffy, like dinner rolls turned vertically, and her titties were small yet palmable with huge brown nipples, the size of green grapes. Tony's dick shot straight to the ceiling as hard as Chinese arithmetic, and she loved it.

He watched intensely as she stood up from the chair, because when she stood up, it looked like she was butt-naked underneath the coat, and he secretly wanted her to be. He felt guilty. He had been thinking about pussy all night long and couldn't wait to see Elaine, but she had texted him and said she wasn't able to come because of work. Right now, though, he was in the company of her friend. Tony tried his best to fight back his lustful desires, but Sarah was doing everything in her power to egg him on. She kept dancing in front of him, making erotic noises and faces, and her body was flawless, everything was in place.

"How would you like some vanilla pudding? It's real sweet," she asked, tasting her fingers after they left her pussy.

He didn't answer. He couldn't answer. He was too tongue-tied by her antics as she traced her finger around her navel piercing. Tony couldn't hold back any longer; she was too irresistible.

"Fuck," he said, looking down at his manhood.

His dick had gotten hard, and there was no way to hide it, he was exposed. Sarah smiled. She dropped to her hands and knees where she stood and crawled across the floor toward Tony, who was lost in lust. She started at his toes, licking, sucking, and feeling him squirm beneath her power again. Sarah worked her way up his legs, and then to his inner thighs sucking lightly, not hard enough to bruise, but hard enough to feel the pressure. Her tongue twirled in circles, flickering in and out like a cobra, leaving moist spots on his body that she blew softly, sending chills up his body.

Sarah ran her freshly manicured nails down the sides of Tony's body hard enough for them not to tickle and let her hands rest on his dick. She toyed with it at first, then gently placed it in her mouth and worked it like a pro. Tony closed his eyes and moaned softly at the job Sarah was doing. It felt so good for a moment, but the guilt wouldn't let him enjoy it because his heart belonged to Elaine. Plus, he didn't want Sarah running her mouth about what happened. He sat up.

"What's wrong?" she asked, staring into his eyes while his dick went limp in her hands.

"As much as I want to, I can't do it," he told her, pushing her away.

"What? What you mean you can't do it?" Sarah asked, getting pissed.

"I'm deeply involved with your friend, and like I said, I can't do it. I love her."

"Fuck that bitch! I don't really like her ass anyway!" Sarah snapped, and Tony saw her agenda for the first time since she'd been in his apartment. She wanted to cause some friction, and he was glad he didn't fall into her trap.

"Naw, baby girl, fuck you! And you can get the fuck out of my crib," he said, standing up.

"At least let me put my clothes on," she said, walking toward his bathroom. Tony didn't object because he wasn't into arguing with her sorry ass.

"Hurry up," he said, fixing the towel.

Tony leaned back on the couch, thinking about what he almost did. In his mind that would have been a catastrophe. He sat on the couch impatient, hoping that Sarah would hurry up and leave. She walked out of the bathroom wearing her coat, gave Tony a crazy look, then headed for the door. He didn't even look in her direction as she exited the apartment, slamming the door behind her.

Tony picked up his cell phone and tried to call Elaine, but it went straight to voicemail. He then grabbed the bottle of liquor he had sitting on the table and took it to the head. The bottle was half empty by the time he removed it from his lips. It left him feeling a bit tipsy. He tried to shake off the dizziness, but the liquor had him zoned out. Suddenly, the door opened again, and with his eyes slowly trying to close, he could see a figure approaching him.

"My fucking head is killing me," he said to himself, placing a hand on his forehead.

The figure walked past Tony then suddenly appeared behind him, yanking his head back. Before he could make a move, he could feel a sharp object running across his throat. It had been slit. Blood began gushing out like a water fountain. He grabbed for his throat, trying to stop the bleeding, but it kept pouring out. The last thing Tony saw before he died was the person that was taking his life. He tried to speak but choked on his own blood.

The killer dropped a small piece of paper onto Tony's lap, then walked out of the apartment, leaving him wondering why. He died a minute later.

CHAPTER NINE

IT TOOK THREE RINGS at the bell before a brass handle turned on one of the antique double doors, painted in glazed red that popped against the creamy neutral stone exterior of the brownstone home. A young woman leaned out of the entryway. With a chic messy bun and airbrushed makeup, she was the type of woman you'd expect to see stepping into an expensive clothing store somewhere.

"Can I help you?"

"Are you Adrianne Benson?"

"Why?" she asked, looking the woman up and down, and then looked like she was waiting for the bad news that usually follows these kinds of visits.

"I'm a reporter, working on a story about the serial killer that's out there murdering innocent people. We need your help, to help the police catch him."

"I don't know how I can help," she said, trying to shut the door, but Elaine did the pesky journalist trick from the movies and stuck her foot in it.

"I'm sorry to bother you at this time," she began. "I know this all has to be really hard on you, losing a loved one, but I just want to know if your father ever talked to you about his work?"

Her face told Elaine that the mention of her father was only making things worse. She looked more angry than sorrowful, but Elaine still needed to know what she knew. She kept her foot in the door until surprisingly, Adrianne opened it up wider and leaned against it.

"My father wasn't all he was made out to be. He was a fucking creep who liked people that he couldn't have, if you know what I mean."

It only took Elaine a second to figure out what she was talking about. "Are you saying that your father was molesting you?" When Adrianne didn't answer, it was all confirmed. "Listen, you were the victim of something that should have never happened to a little girl, but right now, a killer is out there murdering people for some reason, and we need to find out why."

"So what do this have to do with me or my

father?"

"The police are trying to figure out how all these murders are linked, but I don't think they're getting any closer to solving this than they were when it first started."

"Okay, but you're still not telling me what it has to do with us. My father was murdered in the line of duty, when he tried to pull somebody over. From what I was told, the driver opened fire on him, and he tried to call for backup, but they arrived too late."

"Yeah, that's what they want you to think, but I think he was into something else."

"Why are you telling me this? Why haven't the police come to talk to me instead of you? What is your end game in all of this?"

The questions were pouring out of Adrianne Benson like she was the reporter, but Elaine knew that this would happen and was prepared. She answered all her questions and then got some of the answers she needed. Her father was a real predator. Elaine followed Adrianne up the stairs, into the master bedroom, where a huge canopy bed was sitting in the middle of the room.

"I knew about the other women, and to be honest, I knew my dad was dirty. He used to bring home a stack of money and put it in this safe," she said, opening the closet door, revealing a large, black, steel safe. "I learned to deal with it the best I could, and he gave me anything I wanted just to keep my mouth shut."

"After what he did to you, he owed you a whole lot more. It's not your fault, Adrianne," Elaine said, staring at the safe. She wanted to know what was inside. This story was going to make her the best reporter in the world if she solved this case before the cops. Just as she was about to say something else to Adrianne, she received a text message from Sarah.

"Elaine, something horrible has happened. It's your friend Tony. Call me now!"

Elaine immediately dialed Sarah's number to see what was going on. "What happened?" she asked when she answered.

"The police just found Tony's body in his home. He had been murdered," she said, waiting on a response from Elaine.

"How? What happened? Who did this?" she asked Sarah with a distraught look on her face.

"I'll tell you everything when you get here. Meet me at his house. There are a lot of reporters already here, but we have seniority because of who we know. Hurry up and get here."

Elaine ended the call. "Something has come up and I have to go. We will finish this conversation later," she said, handing Adrianne one of her business cards. "Call me later on tonight and we can meet up and finish our conversation." She rushed out of the house, leaving Adrianne wondering what was going on.

~ ~ ~

"How do we know this is our killer?" Eric asked Sonya as he stepped out of his car.

"Because whoever our killer is left another note. I think he's toying with us, Eric. Every time we think we're getting close to him—"

"Or her," Eric interrupted. "Or her!"

"Or her, they seem to get away. This is worse than the Baltimore sniper. How can we catch someone that can't be caught?"

"Easy, we wait patiently and keep working the case. Eventually our suspect is going to slip up, and we'll be there to slap the bracelets on his wrist," he replied as they stepped into the apartment. As they approached Nicole, she was standing there talking with the ME.

"Damn, Detective, what took you so long?"

"My date with your momma lasted all night, and I forgot my toothbrush, so I had to turn around and go back to get it," Eric joked.

"Fuck you, asshole," she said, putting up her middle finger. Both Sonya and Eric smiled. With the ritual ball-busting out of the way, Nicole flipped opened her notepad. "Here's what we have so far. The victim's name is Tony McAndrew. He was forty, and the CEO of *BBB* magazine. His jugular artery was slit open—"

"Wait, did you say McAndrew?"

"Yeah, Tony McAndrew. Why, you know him?"

"Yeah, I know of him. He was dating a friend of mine," Eric replied, then looked at Sonya. "Him and Elaine were together."

"I did hear about that," Sonya said. "Did

anyone let her know?"

"I sent a couple of uniforms over to his company to get statements from his workers," Nicole said. "I also called the news station his girlfriend works at and told them to get ahold of her and let her know."

"Any witnesses, or was anything taken? Maybe it was a robbery."

"No witnesses as of yet, and if the killer was trying to rob him, he really botched it up because absolutely nothing's missing. If there's another reason, we don't know yet."

Eric's gaze moved to the shattered glass that was on the floor from Tony dropping the bottle of liquor. He looked around the apartment, hoping that maybe the killer had left something behind. The Crime Scene Unit tech stared at him for about fifteen seconds, then walked over.

"Don't get your hopes up," Evelyn said. "We already dusted this place for prints. Nothing! If that's not bad enough, whoever killed him knew exactly how to slit his throat with minimum blood splatter. I would think this person was some kind of doctor, or in the medical field. You better get whoever did this before they murder this whole fucking city." Evelyn patted his hand. "Eric, get this creep."

Tony's body was still lying slumped over the couch. He'd fallen in such a way that he was reflected in the ten-foot-high mirror that sat in the far corner. Almost all the blood from his body had spilled out all over the carpet, leaving an uncleanable stain. Eric and Sonya walked over to get one last look at the body. Almost more unsettling than the degree of violence was the shooter's meticulousness. Not only had he been quick and efficient, but he also made sure not to leave any prints at the scene. The killer was good, but we were better.

"We may have a witness, Detective," one officer said, waving his hand in the air. Eric, Sonya, and Nicole walked over to the officer. "The girl on the first floor said someone shoved past her when she was coming through the door. She wasn't really paying any attention, so she didn't see who. She said when she looked up, two people were walking fast down the street."

"What did they look like?" Sonya asked impatiently.

"Not anything like you'd think. They were both dressed in business attire. The man was very well groomed, wearing an expensive tailored suit. White male, around thirty, black hair, six feet, around two hundred pounds, very good looking. The woman was slender, five three, skirt suit, long blond hair, maybe a hundred and twenty pounds, also very beautiful."

The witness's description was crisp, clear, and right to the point. The only problem was, it could be anybody out there.

"Anything on video, like which direction they were heading in?"

"We collected surveillance tapes from the store across the street, as well as a few other places. The witnesses are viewing them as we speak, but I wouldn't hold my breath. There are a lot of people that go in and out of this building every day, all day."

"I'm going to go over and talk to them," Sonya said. "If I get anything, I'll call you."

"I'll tag along if you don't mind," Nicole said.

"See you later," Sonya said to Eric as she and Nicole waved bye and headed out of the apartment.

Eric finished combing the apartment, trying to find anything that could help with the investigation. He looked at the horoscope quote again.

Gemini:

Just when you think you're getting closer, you'll find out that you're only getting further away. Catch me if you can.

The killer was toying with all of them. He or she wanted to be famous. It was at that moment that Eric realized that this person was not going to come in peacefully. They wanted to go out in a blaze of glory.

"I need to speak with someone now," a voice was yelling at the front door. Eric looked over and saw Elaine trying to get past the officer guarding the door.

"Let her through," he said. Elaine pushed hysterically past the officer, trying to get to Tony. Eric grabbed her hand and held her back because he didn't want her tainting the evidence. "Calm down. He's gone, Elaine."

"Noooooo! How? What happened?" she asked, crying in his arms.

"We don't know yet, but I promise you, we're going to do everything we can to find out." He led her back out of the apartment so they could talk. Sarah and her news crew were waiting, along with other reporters, trying to be the first to get the story. "Not right now."

"Eric, we're not here as reporters right now," Sarah lied. Looking at him made her heart beat fast, but she brushed it off. "Elaine's my friend. I'm here to make sure she's alright."

Eric didn't respond. He turned to Elaine, who was still having a nervous breakdown. He helped her over to a chair that a neighbor had brought out and sat her down.

"Is there anything you can tell me about who Tony may have been dealing with? Even though we think this was our serial killer, we think he knew the person who did this. There were no signs of forced entry, which tells us that he let the killer in."

"Tony has been dealing with plenty of people. He's the CEO of a magazine company for Christ's sake," Elaine snapped. "I'm sorry if I'm taking it out on you, but—"

"Trust me, Elaine, I understand. We just need your help if you're able," Eric replied.

For the next few minutes, Elaine tried to help Eric as much as she could. Sarah stood there while her team interviewed residents, trying to pick their brains for information. She was hiding a secret and hoped that no one found out.

CHAPTER TEN

THE RESTAURANT WAS LOCATED on the sixteenth floor of the hotel. It was very trendy and had the most head-spinning views over Ohio.

"Cristal, ma'am?" Jason handed me a glass of chilled champagne as I sat perched on a barstool.

"Why, thank you, sir." I stressed the last word flirtatiously, batting my eyelashes at him deliberately. He gazed at me, and his face darkened.

"Are you flirting with me, Kerruche?"

"Yes, Jason, I am. What are you going to do about it?"

"I'm sure I can think of something," he said, his voice low. "Come with me. Our table is ready." As we were approaching the table, Jason stopped me, his hand on my elbow. "Do me a favor and take off your panties."

Oh? A delicious tingle ran down my spine. He was not smiling, so I figured he was dead serious. Every muscle below my waistline tightened. I handed him my glass of champagne, turned sharply on my heel, and headed for the restroom. In the privacy of the stall, I smirked as I divested myself of my underwear. Here I was out on a date with one of my classmates, and I was in the bathroom, holding my panties in my hand. I always knew he had a thing for me, but he was older and more experienced than I was. When he asked me out to discuss classwork, I knew we wouldn't be doing that, but I wanted to go anyway. He was handsome, so I figured, what the hell? I was glad that I changed into my dress instead of wearing the tight jeans I had on earlier. I hadn't expected the evening to take this unexpected course though.

I was excited already. Why was he affecting me like this? I knew we wouldn't be spending the evening talking about our classwork after what he asked me to do. Checking my appearance in the mirror, I was flushed with excitement knowing that I might get the chance to be with the hottest guy in school. I took a deep breath and headed back out to meet Jason, who was sitting down.

"Sit beside me," he said, standing politely when I approached the table, his expression unreadable. He was looking all calm, cool, and collective. I slid into the seat, and he sat back down. "I've ordered for you. I hope you don't mind."

He handed me my half-finished glass of champagne, regarding me intently, and under his scrutiny, my blood heated up. Here I was drinking champagne at the age of eighteen, and feeling pretty damn good about it. He rested his hand on my thigh. I tensed up and parted my legs slightly, allowing him to touch my wetness. The waiter arrived with a dish of oysters on crushed ice.

"I never tasted oysters before."

"I only had them a few times myself, but they were slamming." He smiled.

"Oh really?"

He took an oyster from the dish, removing his hand from my thigh. I flinched in anticipation, but he reached for a slice of lemon. My pulse was racing. His long skilled fingers gently squeezed the lemon over the shellfish.

"Eat," he said, holding the shell close to my mouth. I parted my lips, and he gently placed the shell on my bottom lip. "Tip your head back slowly," he murmured. I did as he asked, and the oyster slipped down my throat. He didn't touch me, only the shell did.

Jason helped himself to one, then fed me another. We continued this torturous routine until all twelve were gone. His skin never connected with mine. It was driving me crazy.

"So do you like oysters now?" he asked as I swallowed the last one.

"Is that supposed to be a trick question?" I smirked, elbowing his arm.

He placed his hand casually on his own thigh and rubbed his dick. My pussy really started catching fire from the sight of him playing with himself. He ran his hand up and down his length, lifting it, then placing it back where it was. The waiter topped up our glasses and whisked away our plates. His hand moved back over to my thigh, spiking my breathing.

"Damn, I'm really glad you're wearing a dress tonight."

"Oh really?"

"Yes," he seethed. "It makes me want to get under this table right now and eat your pussy until you bust all over your seat, but I'm not going to do that yet."

"Why not?" I asked, getting so turned on that my finger found its way under my dress and squeezed my clit.

"Because, just imagine how you'll feel when I get you back to the room," he whispered. "I can't wait."

"It will be your fault if I combust here in my seat," I muttered through gritted teeth.

"Oh, Kerruche. We'd find a way to put that fire out," he replied, grinning salaciously at me.

I had hardly said a word to this guy in class, and here I was talking sluttishly to him on the first date. It just felt so right, even if it was so wrong. The way he kept looking at me only intensified the lust. I dug into my plate of food, narrowing my eyes in quiet, devious contemplation. I took a bite of the fish. It was melt-in-your-mouth delicious. I closed my eyes, savoring the taste. When I opened them, I began my seduction of Jason, very slowly hitching my dress up, exposing more of my thighs. He paused momentarily, with his forkful of food suspended in midair.

After a moment, he resumed eating. I took another bite of my food, ignoring him. I put my fork down and ran my fingers up the inside of my lower thigh, lightly tapping my skin with my fingertips. It was distracting even to me, especially as I was craving his touch again. He looked at me and smiled.

"I know what you're doing, and it's not going to work," he said. His voice was low and husky. "After we eat and get back to the room, you can have your way with me."

"Who said I wanted you?" I said playfully. He shook his head. I was losing this battle of wills. I glanced up at him again, and his eyes stared back at me. Parting my lips a fraction, I ran my tongue across my lower lip.

"You're something else, Kerruche. I wish I would have noticed you sooner, before I—" He stopped talking.

"Before you what?" I asked, trying to see what he was about to say.

"Nothing! I was just about to say before you met someone else. That's all!"

Keeping my eyes locked on his, I took the spear from my plate and placed it in my mouth, sucking it gently, delicately on the end. The hollandaise sauce is mouthwatering. I bit down, moaning quietly in appreciation. He closed his eyes, and I knew I had him. When he opened them back up, his pupils were dilated. The effect on me was immediate. I groaned and reached out to touch his dick. To my surprise, he used his other hand to grab my wrist.

"Oh no you don't," he murmured softly. Raising my hand to his mouth, he gently brushed my knuckles with his lips, and I squirmed. "Eat the rest of your food. We're not leaving until you're done."

"I'm not hungry anymore. Not for food."

"Just eat a little bit more, and then we'll get out of here." I ate the little bit of mashed potatoes I had left on my plate, then sat my fork down.

"What now?" I asked, desire clawing at my belly. I needed some dick right now, and Jason was going to be my conquest for the night.

"Now? We leave. I believe you had something that needed tended too, and I'm yours for the taking. Let's get out of here. After you, Miss Kerruche." He stepped aside, and I stood up to leave, conscious that I was not wearing my panties.

He gazed at me like he was already undressing me with his eyes. It made me feel so sexy. Deliberately stopping in front of him, I smoothed my dress over my hips. Jason acted like he was whispering in my ear, then squeezed my ass as we exited the restaurant. Waiting by the elevators, we were joined by two other couples that had appeared out of nowhere. When the doors opened, Jason grabbed my elbow and stared me to the back. I glanced around, and we were surrounded by dark smoked-glass mirrors. As the other couples entered, the two men turned and said hi to Jason. He nodded his head but stayed silent.

The couples stood in front of us, facing the elevator doors. They were obviously friends the way the two women were talking loudly and excitedly about what they were about to do. They must have been thinking the same thing I was, 'cause nothing but freaky shit came out of their mouths. I could also tell that they were a bit tipsy.

As the door closed, Jason scooted down beside me to tie his shoes. Discretely he placed his hand on my ankle, startling me, and as he stood back up, his hand traveled swiftly up my leg, skating deliciously over my skin. I had to stifle my gasp of surprise as his hand reached my backside. He moved behind me. I gaped at the people in front of us, staring at the backs of their heads. They were oblivious to what we were doing. Wrapping his free hand around my waist, Jason pulled me to him, holding me in place as his fingers slid inside me. The elevator traveled smoothly down, stopping at the fifth floor to let more people on, but I wasn't paying them any attention. I was too focused on his fingers doing their job.

"Damn, it seems like someone is ready," he whispered as he slid another finger inside my pussy. I squirmed and gasped. I was wondering how he could do this, with all these people here with us. It turned me on even more. "Keep still and quiet."

I'm flushed, warm, wanting, trapped in an elevator with seven people, six of them unaware of our sexcapade going on in the corner. His fingers slid in and out of my hole, again and again. My breathing . . . Jeez, it was embarrassing. I wanted to tell him to stop . . . and continue . . . and stop. I sagged against him, and he tightened his arm around me, his erection against my hip. We halted again at the next floor. I was asking myself how long this torture was going to continue. Subtly I grinded myself against his persistent fingers. After all this time of not touching me in the restaurant, he chose now! Here! And it made me feel sooooo fucking good.

"Mmmmm!"

"Hush," he breathed, seemingly unaffected as yet two more people came aboard the elevator. It was getting really crowded.

Jason moved us further back so we were now pressed into the corner. He held me in place and tortured me even more. He nuzzled my hair. I'm sure we looked like a young couple in love, canoodling in the corner, if anyone could be bothered to turn around and see what we were doing. He eased a third finger inside me. I leaned my head against his chest, closing my eyes and surrendering to his unrelenting fingers.

"Don't cum," he whispered. "I want that later."

Jason splayed his hand out on my belly, pressing down slightly as he continued his sweet persecution. The feeling was exquisite. Finally the elevator reached the second floor. Jason slowly slipped his fingers out of me and kissed the back of my neck. The first two couples that got on with us exited in front of us. We followed behind them.

"Ready?" he asked. His eyes gleamed wickedly as he slipped first his index finger, then his middle finger into his mouth and sucked them. "Tasty, K." I nearly convulsed on the spot.

"I can't believe you just did that," I murmured, practically coming apart at the seams.

"You'd be surprised what I'm capable of doing if given the chance," he replied, reaching out, tucking a lock of my hair behind my ear and smiling.

"You have me so turned on. Now take me to your room and fuck me."

His mouth dropped open, and then he started laughing. I could tell that he was surprised by how loud I had said it, because the couples turned around and looked at us. Jason nodded at them, and the two couples went into the room next to the one we were going into. Once we were inside the room, he pinned me to the wall, and his hand traveled up my leg, his lips intertwined with mine. He hoisted up my dress.

"Wrap your legs around me," he said, lifting me up. He carried me over to the table and sat me down, standing in between my legs.

Reaching into his pants pocket, Jason pulled out a foil packet and handed it to me. He started undoing his zipper, releasing his manhood from its captor.

"Do you know how much you turned me on tonight in that restaurant?"

"What?" I panted. "No . . . I . . ."

"Well you did," he muttered, grabbing the condom from my hands. He ripped the packet open, pulled out the rubber, rolled it onto his penis, and then put his hands under my thighs, spreading my legs wider. Positioning himself, he paused. "Keep your eyes open. I want you to see everything that's about to happen."

Clasping both of my hands with his, Jason entered me slowly. I tried my best to keep my eyes open, but I was beginning to feel dizzy. I thought it was because the dick was so good, but, boy, was I wrong. There was something else going on. The last thing I remembered was the room door opening and the two couples from earlier walking in. Jason was still pumping away when everything went black.

~ ~ ~

The next morning when I woke up, my head was spinning out of control. I felt like I was seeing two of everything I looked at. I was butt-naked, lying on a king-size bed. When I turned over, there were two guys and a woman asleep on the carpet. They were also naked. Upon further verification, I realized that they were three of the people that were in the elevator with me and Jason the night before, but where the hell was he? And why were they in our room? All of a sudden, I had a flashback of what happened last night.

Jason and I were fucking on the table when the two couples came marching in. The guys had on shorts and wifebeaters, and the girls were wearing lingerie. I was so out of it that I didn't know Jason had switched places with one of the guys. The guy was inside me while the girls had removed my dress, and both had a breast in their mouth, sucking on it. Jason and the other guy were watching.

"Oh shit, you are so wet," the guy whispered in my ear. I tried to push all of them off of me, but my arms felt like Jell-O. "Don't fight it, I know you like it."

I tried to adjust my eyes, and when I did, I could see Jason laughing with the other guy as they continued to watch me being fucked by this stranger. I felt his penis jerk inside of me, indicating that he had just released his semen. When he pulled out, he didn't have on a condom. The other guy walked over and switched with the guy that was just humping away inside me. I could see him stroking his massive dick, right before he bent me over and rammed it into me from behind. The pain was so excruciating that it made me pass out.

I shook my head, trying to erase that memory from the night before as I stared at the people on the carpet still sleeping. That's when it dawned on me that I had once again been raped. I was furious because I thought Jason liked me, but he was just like my father and every other man that came around me.

I could hear soft moaning coming from the bathroom. I eased off the bed, stepping over the guy and girl who were spooning each other, and crept over to the bathroom. I put my face against the door and listened. It was Jason, talking dirty to the girl as they fucked.

"Is this how you like it?"

"Yeesssss! Oh shit, harder, faster," she moaned. "Don't stop. You're hitting my spot."

I was so mad that if you sat a teapot on my body, it would start boiling. I slipped my dress back on and eased out of the room before anyone noticed. Revenge was all I could think about as I walked home, and I knew just how to do it.

~ ~ ~

Jason arrived at his dorm room around seven o'clock, tired from the long day he had. He was about to hop on his laptop when someone tapped on his door. As soon as he saw my face, he smiled.

"What's so funny?" I asked, walking in.

"Nothing! I was just thinking about how much fun we had last night. You were really turned the fuck up."

"Nigga, you drugged me," I snapped. "Then you and those guys raped me. Who were they?"

"Wait a minute. What do you mean we raped you? You were just as into it as we were, so don't play that rape card shit."

"Play what rape card shit? Don't come at me

like that. You put something in my drink. I would have never agreed to having an orgy with anyone, especially those people that you had here. What do you think, I'm some kind of slut or something?"

"You said it, I didn't," he smirked.

I decided to flip the script on him, because this conversation wasn't getting anywhere, and he was acting like he did nothing wrong. While he was sitting on the couch, I walked up behind him and started massaging his shoulders.

"Here, let me help you relax," I said squeezing his shoulders. Jason relaxed his muscles while I continued to massage him. "Maybe I did enjoy myself more than I knew I would. It's just that I never did something like that before. This was all new to me. Maybe we should all get together and do it again. This time I'll be a willing participant. Can you call the group of people that were here last night and tell them to join us?"

"Why don't we just have some fun by ourselves? You don't need them here when you have all of this," Jason said, grabbing a handful of his crotch.

"But it would be a whole lot better if we all had fun. This time, I will get to experience the whole thing without passing out like I did last night."

As an incentive, I slid my hand across his chest and down to his genitals. Whatever doubts he had about not wanting to call them over, quickly went out the door. He grabbed his iPhone 11 off the table and texted one of the people. Not even a minute later, he received a reply.

"They're on their way over here right now," he smirked. "How about giving me some head until then?"

"Let's wait until they get here," I told him. "We don't want you to get drained before we even start."

"You right," he replied, reaching back and running his finger across my vagina. As good as it felt, I needed to stick to the plan, so I moved out of his reach.

"I'm going to run to the store real quick. If they get here before I get back, text me," I said, heading toward the door. "You want anything?"

"No, I'm good!" Jason said.

Once I walked out of his apartment, I made my way down to the basement to see what I could find for the next part of my plan. I was able to muster up some ingredients that I could use to make up a concoction that I had found on YouTube. As I was placing the stuff on a table that was located in the corner, I received a message from Jason informing me that our guests had arrived. After mixing everything together just like the video instructed me to do, I made my way back up to the apartment, taking my time, giving them a chance to get comfortable.

When I walked in, the two girls that I remembered from that night were already naked, on the couch, eating each other out, while the three guys watched with their dicks in hand. I smiled.

"I see this party has started. I have to use the bathroom. I'll be right back."

"Don't take too long. After all, this was your idea," one of the men moaned as he continued stroking his dick slowly, making sure I saw him. I walked toward the bathroom, releasing a trail of liquid that was hidden in my purse on my way. When I made it to the bathroom door, instead of going in, I turned the lock on the door, then closed it so no one could get in. I then snuck over to the window and inserted a rubber stopper in the crack so that it couldn't open. Next, I headed over to the door.

"I dropped my weed in the hallway. I'll be right back." They were so preoccupied with the girl-on-girl action that they didn't even pay any attention to me or the liquid pouring out.

I waited outside the door for the chemicals to do their thing. About five minutes later, I could hear people trying to fight the feeling of nausea, then no movement at all. I eased the door open to see two out of the five bodies lying sprawled out on the floor by the bed. Jason and the bitch I heard him with in the bathroom were in the kitchen, lying on the floor. I could tell she had been giving him a blowjob by the way they were positioned. Her head was lying between his legs. The other dude had managed to escape somehow.

The fumes had knocked all of them out cold. I couldn't tell if they were dead or not, and frankly, I didn't give a damn. I searched through everyone's pockets and took all the cash I could find, then grabbed my stuff. Once I made sure I wiped down everything I had touched, I turned on all the burners to the stove, using a dishcloth. I lit a cigarette and placed it on the edge of the stove. Knowing that I only had a minute to get out of there, I picked up my bag and ran from the apartment.

As soon as I was in my car and driving away, there was a loud explosion. I looked in my rearview mirror to see that Jason's apartment was up in flames. Just like with the other people I murdered for doing me wrong, I didn't feel any remorse for the carnage I left.

"We could have had something special, but you crossed me," I said out loud as I put as much distance as I could between me and the bodies left behind.

When I woke up the next morning, it felt awkward that my past kept haunting me. Now I saw what they mean when they say that murders stick with you until you confess. The thing was, ever since I started, I just couldn't stop. I watched from across the street as the same two detectives that thought they were getting close, but weren't, exited the home of my latest victim. I thought it was time for me to lie low, but in my mind, I still had a lot of work to do. "Fuck it. Catch me if you can."

CHAPTER ELEVEN

ALL THE INFORMATION ERIC had collected from Elaine turned out to be unviable for their investigation. This case was starting to be too important to some very powerful people, and they had yet to even be able to put a dent in it. So many questions needed to be answered, and they didn't know where to start. A couple of brass walked into the room where Sonya and Eric were having a conversation and motioned for them to follow behind them.

"I think shit just really hit the fan," Sonya said, setting her cup of coffee down and standing up.

"You can say that again," Eric mumbled.

They were led into the conference room where the mayor, commissioner, governor, and FBI supervisor, along with both Chief Myers and Chief Jones and a few other top officials, were taking a seat. Sonya sat in one of the empty chairs, and as Eric went to sit next to her, Chief Myers stopped him.

"The floor is all yours, Detective," Chief

Myers stated. "Tell us, where are we at on this case, because I'm tired of hearing that you're making progress."

The room suddenly got quiet, and Eric was the center of attention. He was used to this, so he walked over to the podium so he was facing everyone. When he talked, his voice demanded attention, but little did he know, this time his job would depend on what kind of answer he gave his bosses.

"We are following up on a strong lead we think will bring this case to a screeching conclusion. We may have someone in custody by the next couple of days. I know everyone is watching this closely, but let me and my partner do our jobs. We can't possibly do that if we're sitting in this room trying to please all of you."

The look on Chief Myers's face said it all. He was fuming at the way the detective was talking to them. He bounced up, ready to lay Eric out for subornation. Before he could speak, the governor held up his hand.

"So you think that just because we called for this meeting, it's hindering you and your partner from doing your jobs?"

"It came out wrong," Detective Morris said.

"No it didn't," the governor replied. "You said exactly how you felt. And you know what, I admire you for speaking your mind. You're absolutely right; sitting here is wasting precious time that you could be spending out there in the streets trying to catch this killer. So here is something to take with you, Detective. Use all the resources available to you in this room, and get this SOB!"

Eric looked at the governor, shocked. He hadn't expected to hear that come from the big man in charge. He was thinking he would be working behind a desk or directing traffic somewhere by tomorrow.

"I will, sir, thank you!" Eric motioned to Sonya, letting her know that it was time to go. As they headed toward the door, the governor added more fuel to the fire.

"Just remember, if you don't get this guy, that thought you were just thinking a minute ago will only be a figment of the reality you and your partner will endure. You can get back to work now."

"Playtime is over, Eric. They're seriously trying to demote us back to uniforms if we don't find him. I don't know about you, but I refuse to be riding a beat some fucking where," Sonya told him as they grabbed their gear and headed out.

"I agree! But they're just busting our balls, that's all."

"Well I'm not trying to find out if they are or not," Sonya said as she got in the passenger seat. They headed back to the senator's crime scene, hoping they could find something they may have missed.

~ ~ ~

"So you've decided it's time for you and your husband to part company," the divorce attorney said with all the grave emotion the statement and his two hundred-dollar consultation fee deserved.

"But for me, I want to keep my separate account that's in my maiden name," I said, looking professional, wearing a black designer skirt suit. The attorney looked at me as if he thought he recognized my face from somewhere, but he couldn't quite place it. "That's why I came to you. I've heard you're the best at this sort of thing. I don't care how much it costs, either, so long as that man doesn't see one fucking cent of it."

Slowly, ruminatively, Riley leaned back in his cashmere-upholstered office chair. His meticulously designed, oak-paneled office resembled the library of an English country manor, but with extra features. Country manors usually didn't command floor-to-ceiling forty-story views of the city.

"I can assure you that you've come to the right place," he said.

Then he frowned as the light on his interoffice phone began to blink. He had explained emphatically to the temp his one cardinal rule: never, ever, ever interrupt him when he was meeting with a client for the first time. With the amount of money these people spent, they always deserved his undivided attention. Didn't she understand that he was about to make a hefty amount of cash, being that he was one of the most prominent attorneys in Ohio?

The Galaxy on his belt suddenly vibrated, startling him again. What the hell was going on? He glanced down at his cell in annoyance. There was a picture message from an unknown number.

"I'm terribly sorry," he said. "I left instructions not to be interrupted." Riley rolled his eyes as he pulled out his phone to check the message. "If you'll excuse me for just a second."

He opened up the message to see the picture. Below the picture was a written message from an unknown caller: "Remember me, rapist? Now I finally caught up to you!"

Riley stared at the message and picture once more, and then it all hit him. He kept his eyes on the picture, not looking up. Suddenly, he heard a strange coughing bark, and his phone leaped out of his hand.

"Ouch!"

Wiping particles of plastic and glass out of his eyes, Riley tried to focus on me. I was now standing up, with my phone in one hand and my pistol in the other. I tucked the pistol back into my purse and then turned and lifted the little coffee table behind me. It must have weighed no more than sixty pounds, but I reared back and threw it effortlessly through one of the floor-to-ceiling windows. A deafening explosion of shards of flying glass sent Riley to his knees, scrambling to hide behind his desk.

"C'mon, Mr. McCarthy. Don't tell me you didn't think it would all come back to haunt you? How many other girls did you end up raping?" I yelled over the wind that suddenly roared through the office. "You're a serial rapist." Paralyzed, Riley watched legal papers fly off his desk and out the window, all over the pavement and street.

"Noooooo!" he suddenly yelled, making a desperate try to run. He got as far as the edge of his desk before I reached back in my purse, pulled the silenced pistol back out, and shot out both his kneecaps.

The pain was more incredible than Riley had ever believed possible. He tottered to the edge of the glassless window and almost fell through, just managing to wrap an arm around the metal frame. He clung there for dear life, staring four hundred feet down to the concrete and crowds below.

"Here, let me give you a hand," I said, stepping over. "No, hold that thought. Make it a foot." Viciously, I stomped the heel of my shoe into the trembling lawyer's chin.

"Noooooo!" Riley screamed as his grip tore loose and he plunged downward.

"You said that already, fucker," I said with a laugh, watching the body twist and tumble through the last few seconds of its life.

When he smacked the ground, it sounded more like a television set than a person exploding. I strode over to the office door and swung it open. In the corridor outside, I spotted the temp trying to make a call for help.

"Hang that fucking phone up," I said in a low tone. She quickly hung up and raised her hands in the air as if she was surrendering.

"Please don't hurt me. I won't say anything, I swear," she pleaded.

"I know you won't," I replied, putting two

slugs into her chest.

She fell backward into the wall and slid down to the floor. I walked over to the counter and removed a piece of paper from my purse, then dropped it next to her lifeless body. I trotted to the rear stairs with my gun held by the side of my leg, just in case someone else was stupid enough to get in my way. No one else was in sight, though, which made it easy for me to get away without being noticed. I wasn't worried about being caught on camera, because I made sure to hide my face using a sun hat that concealed my identity.

~ ~ ~

Even after a ninety-mile-an-hour ride from the senator's home to the newest crime scene, Eric and Sonya couldn't believe there was another killing already. They screeched up in front of the office building. Behind the crime scene tape lay a lot of glass and one very, very dead lawyer.

"Shot him in the kneecaps first, then must have thrown him," Nicole said as they walked up. "I'm not the biggest fan of lawyers either, but, sheesh." Eric followed her gaze up the sheer glass face of the building to the gaping empty rectangle near the top.

"Any idea how he got away?" Sonya asked, also looking up.

"Came down the service stairs. He had his choice of exits. There're four different ways to get out of here, so he could have used either."

"Detectives, the secretary is still alive," one of the officers yelled as the paramedics rolled her out on a stretcher. "This was next to her."

He passed the paper to Eric, who immediately knew what it was. Another horoscope.

"We have to go; she's lost a lot of blood," one of the medics said.

"I'll go with them," Sonya said. "Our killer finally left us an eye witness. Hopefully she makes it so we can get this person."

"Keep us posted. We'll stay here and process the scene," Eric replied as he and Nicole headed inside the building.

"So, Nicole, tell me, is it true that a bunch of clubs in the city were closed last night because everyone's too afraid to go out?" Eric asked. "Not to mention the waiter over at TGIF who actually stabbed a suspicious customer at lunch because she thought he was the killer."

Nicole shook her head. "This town hasn't been this jumpy since . . . well, not that I can ever recall."

"My sister won't even go out without taking someone with her, and she's one of the bravest women I know," he said, picking something up off the floor. "What do we have here?"

Eric held the object up in the air, staring at it and realizing it was a piece of cell phone, but whose? He searched the area until he found the rest of it. He passed it to one of the CSI workers, who bagged and tagged the device. They had been in the building for a little over two hours now, before Eric's phone started ringing. He pulled it out of his pocket and looked at the screen. It was Sonya. He took a deep breath as he hit the button, guessing that he wasn't going to like what she told him.

"Got anything good for me?"

"Well, that depends," Sonya said. "Our victim

made it out of surgery. She is now resting, but as soon as she wakes up, we'll find out what she knows."

"That's good news, partner. As for us here, I found pieces of a cell phone. I sent it over to the FBI's crime lab to see what they can get off of it. They told us we had all of their resources at our disposal, so I'm going to cash in on it."

"Let me know if they turn up something important, and I will do the same with our vic."

"Will do. Be safe out there," Eric replied, ending the call. "How about we go hound the techs and see what they got?"

"I like your style, Detective." Nicole smiled as they left the office building.

As soon as the two detectives walked through the threshold, they were both bombarded with a barrage of questions from the media. Sarah and her team of cameramen were leading the pack. No matter how much he tried to allude her, Eric just couldn't get away.

"We can't answer any questions right now because this is an ongoing investigation," Eric stated.

"Is it true that the serial killer struck again?" a reporter asked, ignoring what he just told them.

"How long is it going to take for the CPD to catch one person?" Sarah shouted out.

"Why would the killer go after a divorce lawyer? How is all this connected?" another reporter followed up.

The questions were coming at a rapid pace, and Eric nor Nicole had an answer for them. One question, however, did stick out to Eric. It was a question that Sarah had asked. It made him wonder if they were looking at this whole case the wrong way.

"Sorry, but we have to go now," Eric said as they pushed past the reporters. "We'll take my car, and I'll bring you back to yours afterward."

"Okay!" Nicole replied as they hopped in the car.

"I really think we have been looking at this the wrong way. Something's just not adding up," Eric said once they pulled out in traffic. "I think there may be two people involved."

CHAPTER TWELVE

SONYA SAT PATIENTLY OUTSIDE of the room with the two uniformed officers, waiting for the girl to awake from surgery. Her parents were flying in from Philadelphia and should be there soon. She didn't say what really happened to their daughter. She only said that there was an accident. The phone wasn't the proper way to find out that their daughter had been shot multiple times. Luckily, it wasn't worse than it should have been.

"Keep an eye out for anything suspicious while I grab a cup of coffee," Sonya told the young officers on guard duty. They both nodded their heads and stared at her ass as she strutted down the hallway. She knew they were looking too, so she swayed extra hard. "Look but don't touch," she mumbled to herself.

"Damn, I would love to taste that," Officer O'Connor said, shaking his head and licking his lips.

"Who wouldn't?" the other officer replied as she looked into the room to check on the patient.

Officer Kim Elks was bisexual. She loved to play both sides of the field.

"I want to be in the streets, not on no babysitting detail," Chris complained, sitting back down in the chair.

"This is easy money. We'll be back out there soon enough. I'd rather be catching criminals too, but this is what the boss's got us doing, so let's just deal with it."

They were still conversing with each other when an older lady and man came bursting through the double doors. They both had a worried look on their faces. Officers O'Connor and Elks, figuring out who they were, braced themselves for what was about to happen. Sonya walked up just in time to defuse the situation. She pulled the two parents into a side room.

"Detective, what's this all about? What happened to our daughter?" the attractive, fiftyish blond woman demanded sharply, stalking into the room in front of her husband and Sonya. "I would like to see my daughter."

"There was a shooting at her job this

morning," Sonya said. "Your daughter, Erica, was shot multiple times in the chest area. She is recovering safely in the room down the hall. We don't know who is behind it, so we're taking all the precautions to make sure she is safe. That's why there are two uniforms guarding her room."

Catherine's mouth and eyes seemed to triple in size. She stared at Sonya, confused as she stumbled back against her husband, who caught her in his arms.

"Did you catch the son of a bitch yet?" Mr. O'Connor asked, comforting his wife.

"That's why we're waiting on your daughter. We need her to help us get this person off the street. We believe the person behind it has committed multiple other random murders. She is the only survivor so far, and the only one that can identify this person."

"What about the other workers that work there?" Catherine said softly. Her tears stopped like a faucet, and now Sonya could see nothing in her face except rage. "Can't they tell you anything? Why you need her?"

"No one else was in the building that early,

except your daughter and her boss."

"Then I think you should check the video surveillance, because my daughter don't know anything. When she is able to leave, she's coming home with us. We will protect her," James blurted out, being overprotective of his only daughter.

"Whoever was behind it was able to allude the cameras. We can't get their identity. Your daughter is probably the only person that can correctly identify the killer. Sir, we really need her help. Do you understand the severity of this situation? You have my word that I won't let nothing else happen to your daughter."

"I believe you, Detective," Catherine said, then turned to her husband. "I know you want to protect our daughter, James, but it's not our decision to make. If she wants to help them, then let her. If she don't, then she won't. When she wakes up, she'll give them an answer."

The hurt and rage he saw in his wife's eyes softened him up. Sonya could tell his family meant the world to him. Under any other circumstances, she probably wouldn't have pushed so hard, but this was the big break they needed to solve this case, and she couldn't let it slip away. Both her and her partner's jobs depended on it. Mr. O'Connor hung his head, staring at the floor between his sneakers as if trying to read something in the pattern.

"Okay, Detective, do what you need to," he finally said.

"Thank you," Sonya replied, pulling out her phone so she could call Eric and let him know what was going on.

~ ~ ~

"That's awesome news," Eric said, talking to his partner on the phone. "So she's out of the woods, and we're basically just waiting for her to open her eyes."

"How are you and Nicole making out?"

"We are covering some important areas. I will stop past the hospital around nine, and we can speak with her together," he moaned.

"See you then," Sonya replied, ending the call.

"Damn, you almost got me in trouble, girl," Eric mumbled, holding the back of Nicole's head as she bobbed it back and forth on his erection.

They were at Nicole's house, which was only about twenty minutes from the station, having an intimate encounter. The tension had been building between them for a couple of days now, but neither acted on it out of respect for their jobs. What changed all that was the puzzling part. One minute they were working on a case, and the next they were in her bedroom, doing the forbidden dance with each other.

He raised his hand to her face, moving his fingers down her chin, the column of her throat, and her sternum, searing her with his touch, to the first button of her blouse.

"I want to see you," he whispered and dexterously unhooked the button. He planted a soft kiss on her parted lips.

Nicole is panting and eager, aroused by the potent combination of his forwardness, his raw sexuality, and the gentle touch of his hands.

"Oh my," she panted, feeling his hand on her breast.

"Strip for me," he whispered, eyes burning a hole through her clothes.

Nicole was only too happy to comply. Not taking her eyes off of his, she slowly undid each button, savoring his scorching gaze. She saw his desire; it was evident on his face, and between his legs. Her head game had him turned on so bad that he couldn't wait any longer, and helped her out of her shirt. She let it fall to the floor and reached for the button on her jeans.

"Stop," he ordered. "Sit down."

Nicole sat on the edge of the bed, and in one fluid movement he was on his knees in front of her, undoing the laces of first one and then the other sneaker, pulling each off, followed by her socks. Eric picked up her left foot and raised it, planting soft kisses on the pad of her big toe, then grazed his teeth against it.

"Ah!" Nicole moaned as she felt the effect in her groin. He stood up in one swift move, held his hand out to her, and pulled her up off the bed.

"Continue," he said, standing back to watch her do her thing.

Nicole eased the zipper of her jeans down

and hooked her thumbs in the waistband as she sashayed, then slid them down her legs. A smiled displayed on his lips, but his eyes remained dark. It made her feel so sexy, knowing how this man was staring at her. She was wearing white lace panties, with a bra to match. After stepping out of her jeans, she stood there like she was modeling lingerie for him.

Reaching behind, she unsnapped her bra, sliding the straps down her arms and dropping it on top of her shirt that was now on the floor. Next, she slowly eased her panties down her long, thick legs, letting them fall to her ankles, and stepped out of them. Eric looked at her naked body, without saying a word, desire written all over his face.

Besides a couple of stretch marks, Nicole's body was flawless. Eric pulled off his own shirt, followed by his T-shirt, revealing his six-pack. His shoes and socks followed before he reached for his pants. Nicole helped him pull them off.

"I want you so bad right now," Eric whispered in her ear, pulling her into his arms, kissing her neck.

His tongue made its way up to her mouth, where it slid inside, entwining with hers as he walked her backward to the bed and gently lowered her onto it. He lay beside her, pinching her nipples. His hungry mouth found one of her breasts and began sucking on it as his skilled fingers caressed and stroked her clitoris. He moved his hand over her hips and buttocks and down her leg to her knee, the whole time never removing his mouth from sucking her breast.

With her back to him, he slid deep inside her from behind, his fingers tightening around her hair. He began pumping slow, then sped up the pace. The deeper he went, the more Nicole liked it. She closed her eyes and absorbed each stroke. His groans of pleasure had her on the brink of explosion. Her insides began to quiver, and Eric felt her tightening up. That made him speed up even more, going faster and harder. Nicole couldn't hold it any longer and let go, exploding just as he also released his sperm.

"Damn, you just wore me out," she said, leaning back on her pillow. "You want something to drink?"

"No, I have to meet Sonya at the hospital. Our eyewitness should be waking up shortly," Eric replied, putting his clothes back on.

He knew he just crossed a line that may or may not come back and haunt him. It was a consequence worth enduring though. Nicole stayed in bed and watched him as he rushed out the door. Seeing that he didn't even say goodbye, she sent him a text message: "Goodbye to you too!"

Eric smiled when he read it, then sat his phone down as he sped off to the hospital, thinking how good she was.

CHAPTER THIRTEEN

I WENT TO THE KITCHEN and took a bottle of liquor out of the cabinet above the sink. Carrying it in both hands almost ceremoniously, I stepped into the dining room. The corpse was now respectfully arrayed on top of the table that sat inside the floor-to-ceiling glass freezer that I built two years ago, waiting for this moment. I'd washed it multiple times already in the tub, even shampooed and combed the blood and brain matter out of its hair before carefully dressing it in a black suit and tie.

"You are almost ready, my love," I mumbled as if it could hear me. "I just need one last piece to make you complete, and I know just where to find it."

I opened the bottle of liquor and took a long swig, then sat the bottle down on the kitchen table. I pulled out my chrome .380 that was tucked in my side holster and checked the cartridge, making sure it was fully loaded before re-holstering it back in place.

"Once you are complete, you'll be perfect."

I pulled the curtains together to conceal the freezer, then went upstairs to take a quick nap. I figured I needed to be at full strength before completing the last step of my project. I removed all my clothes and hopped into my bed. The three hundred-thread-count sheets felt smooth over my body as I adjusted to the spot I was looking for. I closed my eyes, and immediately, my past once again came to the forefront of my dreams.

~ ~ ~

Sitting in the darkened confessional booth, Father Garrett silently blew his running nose and checked his tiny video recorder. He'd hadn't been sick in over a year, so it came as a surprise that he was now, and at a time like this. Someone had been stealing from the donation box, and the police were no help, so he had to take matters into his own hands to catch them.

Twenty minutes later, he was starting to doze off when he heard a sound—very faint, tentative, a creak that was barely there. Stifling a sneeze, Father Garrett slowly drew open the confessional curtain with his right foot. The noise was coming from the middle aisle's front door! It was opening an inch at a time. Garrett's heart rate kicked into overdrive as a human figure's shadow in the dim glow, emerged from behind it. He watched, mesmerized, as the thief stopped beside the last pew, stuck his arm up to the shoulder down into the box opening, and removed something.

The object was a folder of some kind. So that's how it had been done, Father Garrett thought, watching the intruder slide coins and bills out of the folder into his hand. He'd used a type of retrievable trap that would catch any money dropped in the box. Ingenious. For a petty thief, he was a true mastermind. Except for getting caught red-handed, Garrett thought as he removed his shoes and stood quietly.

In just his socks, so he couldn't be heard, he crept out into the side aisle. He was less than ten feet away from the culprit, approaching silently from behind, when he felt a nasty tingling sensation in his sinuses. It was so fast and powerful that he was helpless to hold it back.

The sneeze that ripped from him sounded like a shotgun blast in the dead silence of the church. The startled figure whirled around violently before bolting for the door. Father Garrett managed to take two quick steps before his socks slipped out from beneath him and he half dove, half fell forward with outstretched arms.

"Gotcha," he cried, tackling the thief around the waist. Coins pinged off marble as the two of them struggled with each other. Then suddenly his opponent stopped fighting.

Garrett got a firm grip on the back of his shirt, hauled him over to a wall switch, and flipped on the light. He stared in disbelief at what his eyes told him. It was a kid, and not just any kid either.

"For the love of God, Sahmeer. How could you?" Father Garrett said, heartbroken. "That money goes to buy groceries for people in the neighborhood that have nothing and can't afford them. But you . . . you live in a nice apartment with a loving family that gives you everything you want, and you do this? Don't tell me you're not old enough to know stealing is wrong."

Sahmeer was a foster child that was adopted

by the Harrison family when he was five years old. He and his sister had been separated because the foster parents only wanted him and didn't want to deal with an almost teenager. The system was flawed and everyone knew it, but chose to look away from the problem instead of trying to find a solution. Hanging around the wrong crowd at school had landed him in the juvenile detention center on more than one occasion, but his foster parents still welcomed him back. His bigger problem was, he wanted his sister. There were plenty of nights that he stayed up on Instagram and Facebook trying to locate her with no success.

He started stealing from anyone he could, trying to get enough money up to run away. In his mind, the only family he had was nowhere to be found, and he vowed to find her. At the age of ten, he had run away multiple times after fighting with the other foster kids. He only had one more chance, or he would be sent back to CPS, but it was a chance he was willing to take.

"I know," Sahmeer said, wiping his teary eyes with his gaze to the floor. "I just can't seem to help it. Maybe my real parents were criminals. I think I got bad blood or something running through my veins."

Father Garrett snorted in outrage. "Bad blood? What a load of bull." He shifted his grip to the young man's ear and marched him toward the door. "Poor Mary must be worried sick about you. You're supposed to be home. You're going to have a sore backside when your father hears about this."

"Please don't tell my father, I'm begging you!"

"I cannot lie to your parents, son. I have to tell them what you've done," Father Garrett replied.

"Noooooo, you can't. I won't let you," Sahmeer yelled.

"Come on!"

As they got closer to the front door, Sahmeer broke free from his grasp and tried to run. When Garrett reached out to grab for him, he slipped and fell, hitting his head on the table. Blood gushed out everywhere from his forehead, scaring the hell out of Sahmeer. He slowly approached Father Garrett as he twitched on the floor, then stopped moving altogether.

"Father," he called out, tapping his shoulder. "Are you okay?"

When he got no response, he panicked and ran from the church. When Sahmeer got home, he ran up to his room and shut the door behind him. Sweat trickled from his forehead, down his face, onto his shirt. He had just caused someone to die. Sitting on his bed, his nervousness turned into relief. The feeling of knowing he had just watched someone die was like a sudden rush. Now he didn't have to worry about his foster parents finding out that he stole money from the neighborhood church.

He pulled out his cell phone and logged into his Instagram account. There were four new messages. Three of them he recognized as friends from school. The fourth one he didn't recognize, because the screen name said I'M HER! Sahmeer opened it up to see who this person was. To his surprise, it was his sister. She had found him. His excitement grew all over when he read the message of how she missed and loved him so much. He immediately sent her a reply back with his cell phone number, and waited.

Sahmeer sat on his bed for almost an hour hoping she'd call him, but to no avail. Disappointment began to set in as he got up to use the bathroom. After washing his hands, he was about to go downstairs to make something to eat, when he heard his phone ringing. He quickly ran back to his room and grabbed it. The caller's name was blocked.

"Hello! Who this?"

"Sahmeer, is this really you?"

He almost choked on his words as tears filled his eyes. "Kerruche, it's me. Where are you?"

"I'm home, Meer Meer," she replied, calling him by the nickname she gave him when they were younger. "I miss you so much. You don't know how long I've been trying to find you."

"I've been trying to find you, too, but my foster parents wouldn't let me," he sobbed. "They said you were with another family in Philadelphia."

"I was, but I came back here to go to college, hoping that I found you. Sahmeer, I came back for you," she told him. There was so much emotion running through both of them that it took several minutes before they spoke again.

"There's so much I need to tell you. I did something bad and I kind of enjoyed it," Sahmeer said.

"Where are you? I'm coming to get you."

"They won't let me leave, Kerruche," he complained. The only way I will be able to leave here is if—" He paused. Kerruche understood what he was about to say. At the age of ten, he was smarter than people thought he was.

"Just tell me where you are, Meer, and I'm coming to get you."

~~~~~~~~~~

When Kerruche arrived at Sahmeer's foster parents' house, he was waiting in the backyard for her. Once they locked eyes, they both ran into each other's arms. The embrace was effortless and magical to them both. It had been a long time coming. Kerruche held him tightly, never wanting to let him go. Sahmeer felt the same way. After what seemed like an eternity, she released him from her embrace and looked him up and down.

"You have gotten so big, lil brother." She smiled.

"I know," he said, waving his head from side to side. "I packed as much of my stuff as I could."

"Come on, let's get out of here," Kerruche said, grabbing one of his book bags.

"Wait! I have to tell you what I did," Sahmeer said, looking worried.

"Sahmeer, we can talk about this in the car. Right now we have to—"

"I killed somebody," he blurted out.

That made Kerruche stop in her tracks. She turned around and looked at her little brother. He was not the person now that she had been separated from a few years ago. Most kids that experience such a tragedy at a young age end up going through some kind of traumatic shock syndrome, but Sahmeer had this look on his face that she knew all too well. She had that same look after she killed her parents. It was the same look she had after murdering Jason and the four people that pulled a train on her. At that moment, she realized that her brother was just like her.

"Sahmeer, what are you talking about? What did you do?"

He told her everything that happened at the church. Kerruche listened to what her little brother was saying, but what intrigued her the most was the fact that he didn't have one ounce of regret for what he did.

"We have to go, Meer Meer. Now," she said, throwing his bag in the backseat of the car. Sahmeer followed behind her and got into the passenger seat. "I won't let anything happen to you again. I promise."

CHAPTER FOURTEEN

"**THE PATIENT JUST WOKE** up and is ready to talk," Sonya said, talking to Eric on the phone.

"Me and Nicole are on our way up now. We just pulled into the parking lot. Do you want some coffee or anything," Eric asked as they exited the car and walked through the double doors.

"A cup of coffee would be great," Sonya replied.

"You got it, partner. See you in a minute." Eric ended the call as they were hopping on the elevator.

He hit the number four on the keypad, and the doors closed. As the elevator headed up, neither of them said a word about what they had done the night before. Eric felt even more guilty because of his new relationship with Sonya. They had become more than just partners now, but how would he and Nicole be able to coexist around her. Only time would tell.

"We are going to have to talk about what

happened at some point," Nicole said, breaking the ice as they stepped off the elevator.

Eric stopped by the nurses' station to grab a cup of coffee for Sonya. Just as he was about to answer her, gunshots rang out and people began to scream. Removing his gun from his holster, Eric pushed against the fleeing crowd of nurses, doctors, and pedestrians, hearing two more shots and realizing they were coming from the direction where Sonya and the eyewitness was located. Nicole had figured it out as well, as she also had her gun in hand, aimed at the ready.

They split on each side of the wall, ignoring the people bolting for cover, trying to locate the shooter. There was a pause, then two more shots.

"Get out of here," Eric yelled at the security officer who was trying to help them. "Get everyone off of this floor."

They made it to the end of the hall, and Nicole peaked around the corner. Her face almost immediately screwed up.

"Two wounded," she hissed. "One is the

officer that was guarding the room."

"How bad?" Eric whispered, hoping his partner was okay. "Any signs of Sonya?"

"No sign of her yet, but there's blood all over the floor. Looks like the officer took one in the leg and torso area. He's sitting up against the wall with a big pool under him. He may be unresponsive."

"Femoral?"

Nicole took another look and said, "It's a lot of blood."

"Cover me," Eric said. "I'm going to try and pull him to safety."

Nicole nodded. Eric squatted down and crawled out in the open, half expecting some unseen gunman to open fire. He made his way towards the officer who was barely breathing, then grabbed him by the shirt and started pulling him to safety. Nicole scanned the area looking for a target, but no one fired. There was no movement at all coming from that end of the hallway. The injured officer's eyes were open and bewildered. His head was slumped to the side, but Eric could see that he was still breathing, which was a good thing.

"Hold on, okay? Help is on the way, Officer . . ."

"Randle, ma'am. My . . . name . . . is . . . Corey Randle," the officer stated, choking on his words.

"Be patient, Corey. It's gonna be okay!" Nicole replied. "Eric?"

She observed a serious gunshot wound to his lower thigh. A needle-thin jet of blood erupted with every heartbeat. They knew if they didn't get him some medical attention quick, he may die on the scene. By them being in a hospital, you would think it would be easy, but they had evacuated the floor, and there wasn't a doctor around to help.

"Call it in," Eric ordered as he removed his belt and wrapped it around the officer's upper thigh, clinching it tightly. "That should hold for now."

"This is officer Carson, badge number 7609. We need backup at the Cleveland emergency room. There's an active shooter still in the building. Be advised that there are multiple casualties. Plainclothes officers are on the scene," Nicole said, calling it in to dispatch.

The blood stopped squirting. Eric looked up at Nicole, who had just finished making the call to dispatch as she continued to look around for the shooter.

"I'm going to find Sonya and the witness," Nicole said, heading in the direction of the room.

"Did you see who the shooter was?" Eric asked the officer, trying to help him relax a little.

His eyes blinked open and stared up at Eric, disoriented for a moment, before his attention strayed past him. The officer's eyes widened, and the skin of his cheek went taut with terror. He tried to speak, but the words wouldn't come out. Eric immediately caught on to what he was trying to say. He snatched his weapon up and spun around, raising it in the direction the officer was looking. He saw Nicole with her back to him, gun aimed low, peeping in the room next to the one his partner should have been in. All of a sudden the hallway lights went out.

Someone was creeping up on her from the other side of the hallway. The assailant was crouched in a fighting stance in the doorway. In their crossed arms were two nickel-plated .40 cals, one aimed at Nicole and the other at Eric.

With all the training he'd been lucky enough to receive, you'd think he would have done the instinctual thing for a person facing an armed assailant and yelled "gun" to Nicole. But for a split second, it didn't register fast enough because he was too stunned by the fact that he knew the shooter. In that same instant, the assailant fired both guns. Traveling less than thirty feet, the bullet hit Eric so hard, it slammed him backward. His head cracked off the concrete, and everything went just this side of midnight, like he was swirling and draining down a black pipe, before he heard a third shot and then a fourth.

Something crashed close to him, and he fought his way toward the sound, toward consciousness, seeing the blackness give way, disjointed and incomplete, like a jigsaw puzzle with missing pieces.

"Oh, my head."

Five, maybe six seconds passed before he

found more pieces and knew who he was and what had happened. Two more seconds passed before he realized he'd taken the bullet square in the Kevlar vest that covered his chest. It felt like someone had taken a sledgehammer to his ribs and a swift kick to his head. In the next instant, Eric grabbed his gun and looked for . . .

Nicole was sprawled out on the floor about twenty feet away from where he had been lying. Her slim body looked crumpled until she started twitching electrically, and Eric saw the head wound. Blood gushed out like a fountain.

"No!" Eric shouted, becoming fully alert and stumbling over to her side. He couldn't see the shooter.

Nicole's eyes were rolled up in her head and quivering. Eric placed his hand over the hole in an effort to stop the bleeding, but it wasn't working. Suddenly, there was a whizzing sound, and he felt a sting in his neck, then a bolt of electricity running through his veins. His gun fell out of his hand. He tried to reach for it, but a shoe kicked it away. Eric tried to get his composure, and then he heard two shots. He looked at Nicole's lifeless body as blood poured from the newly opened holes around her heart area. The assailant stood over Eric.

"You were getting too close."

"So what are we going to do about him?" another voice said, causing Eric to turn in that direction. His eyes were still fuzzy, so he couldn't see who the other person was.

"He has the last piece I need. Sorry, Eric," the assailant said, then cracked him in the head, knocking him unconscious.

~ ~ ~

Pale morning fog shrouded much of the cemetery from Eric's view. The fog swirled on the wet grass, the melting snow that remained, and gravestones. It left droplets on the pile of wilted flower bouquets that sat over the gravesite. Eric tried to move but couldn't.

"You're not going anywhere, so get comfortable," the familiar voice said, causing Eric to remember what happened before he was knocked unconscious. "I know you have a lot of questions. Maybe I'll answer them, maybe I won't."

They were inside an indoor mausoleum that was made of all glass so people could see the gold casket that sat inside. Eric was semiconscious now, and once he was able to focus, he looked right into his abductor's eyes. What he saw made him somewhat distraught. There was a lot of pain and heartache behind them. Eric was tied down on a table of some sort, and right next to him was the open casket. Inside were the bones of the person that once occupied it. Eric needed to focus on getting loose.

"So all this time we were running around, searching for a serial killer, you were right under our nose," Eric said, trying to shake off his headache.

"Make sure you get it right," the other person in the room added. "*We*, were right under your nose."

"Why are you doing this, Sonya?" Eric asked the person he thought was his partner.

"The question you should be asking yourself is, what's about to happen to you?" she replied, holding a sharp scalpel in her hand. "And my name is not Sonya, it's Kerruche."

Eric gave her a strange look, wondering what she was talking about. He wasn't comprehending what she said, so he just stared at the person that he believed to be his partner and possible future soulmate. After about ten seconds, he finally spoke.

"Is this some kind of fucking joke?" he said, trying to break free. The restraints were so tight that they were cutting off the circulation in his wrists and ankles. "What do you mean your name is Kerruche?"

"Don't look at me like that, partner. You heard exactly what I said. Since you'll be dead soon, I'll explain."

~ ~ ~

"How can I help you?" the court clerk asked.

Kerruche and Sahmeer turned around and in the direction of the beautiful female standing behind the large desk. She wore a burgundy suit skirt that fit her to perfection, and a white blouse that exposed her breasts. The glasses she wore made her look like she was from one of those naughty *Girls Gone Wild* videos. She wasn't wearing the proper attire you would wear working in a courthouse. Kerruche knew that by the way most of the male employees lusted over her as they walked past, and the disgusting looks the females gave her. She was the one they came to see.

"I talked to someone over the phone about getting me and my little brother's names changed. They said we had to fill out the application online and then come see you to go over the paperwork," Kerruche told the female who was staring at her like she wanted to rip her clothes off.

"I can help you with that," she replied, pulling up a different screen on her computer. "I will need both of y'all's current names, birthdates, and social security numbers so I can pull up your applications and run an NCIC check to make sure neither of you have any warrants or outstanding debts."

"I was hoping you could just approve our paperwork without the checks," Kerruche said, giving her a seductive stare and placing a large amount of cash on the counter in front of her.

The court clerk took money to do off-the-book jobs for people who needed them. Not to mention, from time to time she would occasionally bed the same sex. Kerruche knew all this because her friend had told her. All she had to do was flirt with her a little and show some money, and the clerk would make it happen. At this point, she would do anything for her brother.

"How about we discuss this when I get off work?" the clerk asked, licking her lips.

"We really need this done ASAP! Is there anything I can do right now to make you change your mind?"

"Maybe you can," the clerk replied, tucking away the money.

A couple minutes later Kerruche and the clerk were in a bathroom stall, and she was on her knees, licking on the clerk's vagina. It didn't take long before she was exploding all over Kerruche's lips. Her knees were shaking uncontrollably as she held on to the sides of the stall. Kerruche smiled, squeezing the clerk's ass as she sucked up her juices.

"You were great," the clerk said, pulling down her skirt.

Kerruche stood up, wiping her mouth with some toilet tissue, then unlocked the stall door. The clerk followed her out as they washed their hands at the sink.

"So do we get our new identification now?"

"After that performance, how can I say no? Is there anything else you need?" the clerk said, typing something on the computer screen.

"These IDs can't be traced back to us, right?"

"No, they cannot. Now, I need both of you to stand in front of that camera, one at a time so I can take your picture for the ID cards."

Kerruche went first, posing for the camera like a model. An hour later, she and Sahmeer had their new identities. While the clerk was busy finishing up with the paperwork, Kerruche slipped a crushed-up substance into the clerk's food and drink that sat on the desk. She was oblivious to what was happening. Once they finished up at the DMV, they headed out to look at a new home, located on Superior Lane. Kerruche's new name was Sonya Lee, and

Sahmeer's was Samad Lee.

A couple years later, Sonya became a Cleveland police officer, training with one of the best tactical teams in the state, while Samad continued going to school with the hopes of studying medicine when he was old enough for college. He watched all the doctor and CSI shows that came on television, mostly paying attention to how people were murdered and what was used to do it. He also had a fetish for watching how autopsies were done. It, in its own disgusting way, turned him on. It didn't take Sahmeer long before he was trying it himself.

When Sonya realized what her brother was in to, she did everything in her power to keep him safe from apprehension. Knowing that most of the murders in the city were her brother's own doing, she joined homicide so she could keep tabs on them. It made it easier for him to keep doing what he was doing. At first it started off as killings with a purpose. Anyone did something to a child was fair game in his eyes. It didn't matter if it was harmless or not. If he went into a store and a parent was hitting their child in front of a crowd, he felt like it was a form of disrespect, and they were punished for it. The punishment was death. Then the killings became random as it turned into a thrill for him.

One day Sonya's world came tumbling down when she stumbled across a gruesome crime scene that changed her way of thinking. Her best friend Russell's jealous girlfriend caught him in bed with another woman and shot both of them multiple times, then decapitated their bodies. Sonya was one the first to arrive at the scene. She had been in love with him since they met at one of their training seminars, but never got the chance to tell him how she felt.

That's when she met Eric. He came in with such a swagger that she was immediately drawn to him. He was from another district and had transferred in because he needed a change of venue. He was tired of working with people he couldn't trust. That was one of the biggest problems that occurred with people that were still stuck in the '70s. Eric was an African American detective who was on the rise at a rapid pace, and there were many that resented that. His knack for solving crimes was impeccable.

Their boss matched them up to solve the case. Since they already knew who the suspect was, it was open and shut quickly. The two complimented each other, and it was the beginning of their partnership. Sonya still thought about Russell and how she never got to tell him how she really felt.

As time passed, Sonya's feelings for Russell started to trickle over to her partner. She hated seeing him with female after female. Every time he would come back from his days off, he would tell her about some random chick that he met at the bar. Even though Sonya had her share of men, she still couldn't see herself settling with just anyone. She had to have the perfect guy. Sonya's jealousy started really taking its toll one night when she headed over to Eric's house to tell him how she felt. When she turned up his block, she saw him kissing on some woman as they stood in the doorway. Her rage kicked into overdrive, causing her not to think clearly.

She kept on driving by them. She drove

around looking for trouble and found it. A man was pissing in an alleyway as Sonya rode by. She stopped her vehicle and jumped out to confront him. As he tried to run, Sonya pulled out her backup weapon and fired, hitting him twice in the back. He fell down in a puddle of water and piss mixed. That was the first time she killed someone as a cop, and she enjoyed it. Some of her rage subsided as she hopped back in her car and pulled away. In her mind, being a police officer had its perks. That night triggered her past to come back up, and it became the start of her killing spree.

With help from her brother, she decided to build the perfect man on her own. Not thinking it through, she would amputate a part of each person she killed and use it to start her project. Her brother, on the other hand, just killed for the fun of it. Sonya wanted her killings to stick out, so she periodically left different horoscopes on the victims' body for the police to try to solve. In her mind, she was smarter than everyone else. Eric was the last piece of her masterpiece.

~ ~ ~

"So, Eric, as you can see, this storm's been brewing for quite some time now," Sonya said, snapping back to the present.

"And it's a storm that will never reach the surface," Eric retorted. "Let me go now, and there's a chance that you will only get the death penalty by lethal injection. If you don't, I can assure you, partner, that it won't end well for you or your brother."

"Fuck you," Samad screamed, then punched Eric square in the jaw. "We'll take our chances." He walked out of the mausoleum.

Eric's jaw felt like putty as he tried to shake off the pain. From the impact of the blow, he knew that it was broke. All the police training in the world couldn't prepare him for what he was about to see. When Samad came back in, he was wheeling a stretcher. On top of it was a black body bag that contained a corpse. Eric's vision wasn't fully a hundred percent yet, but his eyes definitely weren't deceiving him when he saw what was inside.

"Don't look so disgusted. I'm trying to create the perfect man, and guess what?" Sonya said, rubbing the back of her hand across his face. "You are just that."

The dismembered frame had different human body parts that were sewn together, creating a human. The only thing that was missing was the head. It was something out of a Frankenstein movie. Puke tried to make its way into his mouth, but Eric swallowed hard.

"You're one sick bastard," Eric blurted out.

Sonya placed the knife to his neck. "Don't worry, it will be over quick."

"Wait, wait," he said, pleading for his life. "Look, Sonya, don't do this. We've known each other for years, and this is not you. Sonya, look at me. Look at me, please! I fell in love with you even before we spent that night together. Can't you see, you don't have to pretend to have me. You already have me."

"He's lying, Sis. Let me do this muthafucka," Samad said, walking toward Eric. Sonya held up her hand, stopping him.

"I got this. You have helped me enough, and it's time to say goodbye."

"What are you talking about?" Samad asked,

confused.

"I'm sorry for this."

Before Samad knew what happened, Sonya jammed the knife deep into his heart, twisting it to open the wound. He grabbed for his chest. His eyes were in disbelief as he fell over to the floor. Blood poured out from his body.

"I love you," Sonya whispered, then turned toward Eric.

He didn't know what to expect next, now that he just witnessed her killing her own brother. All he knew was that he better pray he was getting through to her. If not, he was surely the next to be slaughtered.

"Sonya, I love you and would do anything to prove it to you. Believe me, I can love you better alive than I can dead. That right there," he said, pointing to the corpse, "is not me. My body is the real thing. Don't do this!"

"Shut up! Shut up!" Sonya yelled, closing her eyes and covering her ears. "I don't want to hear it. They made me this way."

"Who made you this way, Sonya?"

"It doesn't matter now. They're all dead."

Nothing was making sense to Eric. He didn't know what or who she was talking about. The restraints around his wrist were still too tight for him to get out of by himself. He needed to come up with a plan to get her to release him. All this time together with Sonya, and he never saw her act like this. She was like a woman possessed, and Eric was her Svengali.

"Sorry, but I need you to take a nap until I return," Sonya stated, sticking him with a needle. The drug was instantaneous, sending Eric into la-la land. "Sleep well, handsome."

CHAPTER FIFTEEN

THIS TIME WHEN ERIC woke up, it wasn't daytime anymore. Night had landed, and the only light he could see was from the moon outside and the lamp that was hanging from a metal wire. There was a heater in the corner of the mausoleum that kept it warm. Once again he had a splitting headache due to being drugged. When he turned to his right, Sonya was watching as some kind of crimson liquid was being transferred from an IV bag into the made-up corpse's body. A closer look, and Eric realized that the bag of liquid was blood. Once he was able to focus, he couldn't believe his eyes. Instead of using his head, Sonya had decapitated her own brother's head and attached it to the body.

"I took into consideration what you said, and I want you to show me just how much you love me. Don't fuck me over, Eric, or you will be sorry."

Eric stared at her momentarily and saw

nothing in her once beautiful eyes. This was not the person he had known all these years. Anything he had to do in order to stay alive, he would do. The main focus was getting out of those restraints.

"Sonya, you are my world. Come over here, and I'll show you how serious I really am," he told her, hoping she would fall for it. In order for his plan to work, he needed at least his hands free.

Sonya switched the blood bags that she had stolen from the county morgue, then walked over to the table where Eric was lying. She gave him a rough kiss on the lips, biting on his bottom lip until she tasted blood. He squinched in pain.

"I want you to make love to me," Sonya said, unbuttoning her khaki pants and pulling them off. She then stepped out of her laced panties, leaving them on the cement floor. "I want to feel you inside of me again."

She unhooked Eric's belt buckle, unsnapped his pants, and pulled them down along with his boxers to his ankles.

"You can at least release my hands."

"Okay, but only one," Sonya replied, releasing his left hand.

Eric started to protest, but thought about it. One free hand was better than none. He looked around for anything he could use as a weapon, but there wasn't anything. He didn't know what she had done with his guns, or hers, for that matter. However, one thing he did know was that she wouldn't hesitate to kill him, evidenced by what she had done to her brother.

Sonya got on top of him, lowering her body onto his semi-erect penis. As much as Eric tried not to enjoy it, he couldn't ignore the warm feeling of her wet pussy. His dick immediately responded by hardening all the way up. Sonya began moving up and down as he cupped one of her breasts with his free hand.

"Oh, yes! I wanna have your baby," Sonya moaned with her eyes closed. "If you love me, get me pregnant."

"Only if you free my other hand," he mumbled loud enough for her to hear.

Sonya stopped in mid-stroke, and hopped off of him, looking down at him. "What do you think,

I'm stupid or something? You want me to release your other hand so you can kill me, Eric?"

"No, baby, I want to be able to touch you like I want. That's all, baby!"

Thinking the worst, he tried to calm her down. It worked momentarily. She grabbed her pants and slipped them back on. By her demeanor, Eric knew something wasn't right. Had he fucked up his only chance of getting out of there alive? He didn't know.

"I knew you were like the others. You wait right there, I'll be back," she said, shaking her head in a hysterical manner. She stormed out of the mausoleum, forgetting to tie his hand back up.

Knowing that Sonya would return any minute and that this was his only chance, Eric jumped into action. He began struggling with the restraints, trying to get himself free. Once his other hand was out, he started working to free his ankles. What seemed like minutes was really only seconds, as the restraints were off and he was up on his feet

"This bitch is going down," he mumbled to himself.

Sonya walked back in and noticed Eric wasn't on the table. She dropped the bag she had retrieved from her vehicle, and immediately reached for her gun. As she scanned the area in search of Eric, she didn't see him creep out from under the casket. She turned just as he was about to grab her. Sonya swung her gun up at Eric and fired. He threw his arm out just in time, slapping it away. The bullet hit his shoulder.

Eric gasped and tried to swing at her with his injured arm, missing her. He trained her, so he knew she was an expert at hand-to-hand combat. With his other hand, Eric grasped a handful of her hair and wrestled her toward the glass wall. They both fell to the ground, clawing and struggling. Eric gained leverage because he was stronger than she was and put his knee on her chest. He twisted the gun out of Sonya's hand—with the bullet wound, there was very little strength in his arm.

Sensing that he was hurting, Sonya used

that to her advantage, lifting her leg and wrapping it around his neck. With her other leg, she kicked at the gun, knocking it out of his hand. It slid across the floor. Knowing that his life was on the line, Eric punched Sonya square in the jaw trying to knock the fight out of her, but she was relentless. She kicked him up in the air, then lunged for the gun. Eric knew he had to make a run for it, but he wasn't going to let any woman beat him. They both went for the gun. Sonya reached it first and aimed it at Eric, firing.

He staggered backward, feeling an explosive burning in his abdomen. She aimed again and fired. The bullet went wild, so close that he could hear it whining next to his ear like a supersonic insect. Eric somehow managed to dive through the door of the mausoleum, onto the gravel of the cemetery. Sonya was right behind him. As he made it to his feet, three more bullets flew past his head. The punch to her face threw her aim off.

"Fuck," she yelled, chasing after him. "Come back here. I will find you."

Eric crawled up behind one of the

tombstones and leaned against it. The darkness helped hide his location even though he had left a trail of blood behind. His stomach lurched, and he retched up red-hot liquid that tasted like copper. He thought for a moment about how the hell he was going to get away from this psycho. One thing he couldn't do was let her get away. He inspected the wound: a dark hole the size of a dime to the left of his navel. There was no exit wound, meaning the slug was sitting somewhere in his belly. His body started to shiver violently. He was hoping some passerby heard gunshots and called the cops.

Eric was thinking that if he could get to her car, maybe he could find her cell phone, if she didn't have it on her, or the keys would be in the ignition. In his condition right now, she had the upper hand. Even though he was a lot stronger than she was, the gunshot wounds were taking a toll on him. He needed to get some medical attention soon. His entire body was enveloped in a warm numbness. All he could do was sit in the puddle of his own blood and wait for her to find him so he could kill her. Or she would kill him. Whichever came first.

~ ~ ~

Sarah sat in front of her computer monitor. The whole article was there on her screen, perhaps her finest piece of investigative journalism to date. She had been trying to get back in Eric's good graces by checking on old murder cases that would maybe help solve this one, when she stumbled across one that caught her eye. It was a case about two foster parents that were murdered. What caught her attention was one of the kids that was there. The young girl looked so familiar, which drove Sarah to do some deeper digging. What she found out damn near knocked her out of her chair.

"It's amazing what you can find on the internet."

"What happened?" one of the other reporters asked.

"It may be nothing, but take a look at this," she said, showing him the screen. "That is Eric's partner. She changed her name illegally, and I guess they thought it was gone for good, but nothing's never gone from the internet. You can find anything if you search hard enough."

"Does he know?"

"I'm not sure, but I think I should let him know."

"What does it have to do with this case though?"

Sarah spent the next ten minutes showing him the past murders and how they were killed. She showed him how similar they were, and even though she was young, she seemed to be in the vicinity of all of them.

"What if she knows more about these murders than she's letting on? Why would she keep the fact that she changed her name a secret? Before you answer that, I checked into that also. A young boy had been declared missing back around that time, and after some extensive searching, I found out that it was her brother. What if they changed their names because they didn't want anyone to find out who they were?"

"Then I think that you should tell Eric and let him worry about it. He is the police, and you are only a reporter, so act like it, and report it," her friend said, smiling.

Sarah tried calling Eric's phone several times, and it kept going straight to voicemail. She then called the station, and they hadn't heard from him since the day before when he was supposed to go question the vic at the hospital with Nicole. That set off an instant alarm in Sarah's head. One thing about Eric, he was married to his job. If he wasn't there, he was at his apartment.

She jumped up from her desk and headed out to the parking lot. She drove over to Eric's home, feeling a compulsion to tell him in person about her discovery. When she got there, the lights were out and no one was home. She didn't understand what was happening because she never experienced something like this before.

Then she remembered something they did when they went to a concert and lost each other. They had installed a friend finder on each other's phone so they would be able to find one another the next time. She pulled it up, and the last location was near a cemetery. Sarah wondered why he was there at this time of night, then thought that maybe he went to visit a loved one and didn't want to be bothered. Because this was an emergency, she decided to go there.

~~~~~~~~~~

Eric was beginning to lose consciousness because of the rapid amount of blood he was losing. Even though it was cold outside, he was sweating profusely. Looking around, he realized that he must be deep in the middle of the cemetery because he couldn't even see a road anywhere.

He could hear footsteps approaching and readied himself. He would not be dying tonight without putting up a fight. There was a rock close to where he was sitting. He picked it up and prepared to throw it at whoever was coming. The light from a flashlight was just a few yards away. Eric, still hurting from being shot, got up in a ready stance as if he was about to run in a track meet.

The light got closer. Closer. Eric gripped the rock, ready to charge. Closer. As soon as the footsteps were within arm's reach, Eric used all the strength he had within his body to lash out in an effort to defend himself.

He swung the rock as hard as he possibly could, hitting Sonya in the arm that held the gun, causing her to fall to the grass. The gun fell out of her grasp again, and Eric kicked it away. Sonya was quicker, doing some kind of swing kick, sending Eric to the grass also. In his mind, this fight was over if she found that weapon. Doing the best he could, Eric made it to his feet and charged Sonya again. She sidestepped his move and countered with one of her own, gripping his injured arm and flipping him to the ground.

"Ahhhhh," Eric screamed when she dug her thumb into the bullet hole.

She wrapped a rope around his neck and started pulling it tightly, in an effort to strangle him. Due to all the pain he had been enduring, he couldn't fight any longer. He was submitting to what he thought would be a quick death.

Suddenly, there were two gunshots, and then Sonya released the grip around his neck. She slumped to the ground. Eric tried to look up, but his vision was blurry. All he could see was a silhouette of someone standing there holding a gun. He could hear sirens in the distance getting closer and closer and knew that someone had finally called the cops and they were here to save him.

"Eric, can you hear me? Hold on, help is on the way," Sarah distraughtly told him, bending down to comfort him until help came.

When she first arrived at the cemetery to tell him about what she had discovered, she heard two people fighting about something. After calling the police, she eased her way through the dark cemetery. She could see a flashlight, and what appeared to be a gun being kicked away as they continued to tussle. She noticed that Eric was in trouble, and if she didn't do anything, Sonya would kill him. Never shooting a gun before, she grabbed it and fired with no hesitation. The first shot went wide, but the second one found its target, hitting Sonya in the back.

"Thank you!" Eric managed to mumble before passing out.

Epilogue

Eric had been floating in darkness so pure that it felt like death. Then he woke up! His heart thumping like a kick drum, his skin clammy and hot. He thought he was dead. He was lying in a hospital bed with dozens of medical staff and law enforcement agencies standing outside the room talking. There were flowers and get-well cards sitting on the nightstand beside him. Eric wondered how long he had been out.

When he tried to sit up, he felt a throbbing pain in his stomach. He looked down and saw white bandages stretched across his abdomen. He noticed for the first time that there was an IV coming from a machine that was hooked to the bed. It was feeding fluid into his arm. Eric swung his feet off the bed and onto the floor. He had only a hospital gown and boxers on, with nothing else.

His mouth was dry, so he snatched a plastic water container from the nightstand and drank it down. After finishing off the water, he yanked the IV needle out of his arm. A nurse came rushing into the room as he tried to stand up. His legs were weak.

"Mr. Morris, you have to rest. You suffered an enormous amount of blood loss, and you're still very weak."

"I need to get out of here," he snapped. The last thing he remembered was someone saving him from being killed. It was Sarah. "Where is Sarah?"

"Your friend went home to change clothes, but she should be back anytime now," the nurse replied.

Just then, Chief Jones, Chief Myers, Agent Cezare, and the mayor, along with other brass, came into the room to see how Eric was. They were glad to see him awake and moving about.

"How are you feeling, Sergeant?" Agent Cezare was the first to say.

"I could be doing better. How long have I been out?"

"Almost twenty-five hours," he said.

"Do you remember anything at all about what happened to you?" Chief Myers asked. "We know your partner was involved."

"Where is she? She's the killer," he said.

"Why didn't I see the signs?"

"No need to worry about her, Eric. She is lying in the county morgue right now. After you answer some questions, I want you to get some rest, then take a nice long vacation. That's an order."

Eric gave his boss an affirmative smile. They videotaped him as he gave them his account of everything that happened leading up to the death of Sonya Lee. As they were exiting the room, Sarah came in. She walked over to his bedside.

"Again, thank you for saving my—"

"Shhhh, don't say it," Sarah said, placing a finger over his lips. "I love you, Eric Morris."

This was new to him. He was so used to having one-night stands, that love wasn't in the plan. He wouldn't let himself get emotionally attached to anyone. It took him by surprise that she said it so abruptly, but at that moment, he was all in. He gave her a passionate kiss, then looked her in the eyes with a serious face.

"I love you too!"

~ ~ ~

Nine months later, Sarah became Mrs. Sarah Morris, and they were expecting their first child any time. They were waiting for the papers to be finalized on their new home, but for now Eric's place would have to do. Sarah didn't mind where they stayed, as long as they were together.

"The doctor said that if the contractions get worse, come back in," Sarah said as they sat at the light. She was holding his hand. "Are you happy about the baby?"

"Happy as I'll ever be," Eric replied.

As the light turned green, Eric was easing out into traffic when a Mack truck ran a red light, smashing into their car. They struggled to get out, but the doors were jammed shut. Gas leaked out onto the street.

"Help! My baby," Sarah screamed, grabbing at her stomach.

"The door is stuck," Eric yelled. Seconds later, the car erupted in flames, killing everyone in it.

To order books, please fill out the order form below:
To order films please go to www.good2gofilms.com

Name:_____

Address:_____

City:_____State:_____Zip Code: _____

Phone:_____

Email:_____

Method of Payment: Check   VISA MASTERCARD

Credit Card#:__ _____

Name as it appears on card: _____

Signature: _____

Item Name	Price	Qty	Amount
48 Hours to Die – Silk White	$14.99		
A Hustler's Dream - Ernest Morris	$14.99		
A Hustler's Dream 2 - Ernest Morris	$14.99		
A Thug's Devotion – J. L. Rose and J. M. McMillon	$14.99		
All Eyes on Tommy Gunz – Warren Holloway	$14.99		
Black Reign – Ernest Morris	$14.99		
Bloody Mayhem Down South – Trayvon Jackson	$14.99		
Bloody Mayhem Down South 2 – Trayvon Jackson	$14.99		
Business Is Business – Silk White	$14.99		
Business Is Business 2 – Silk White	$14.99		
Business Is Business 3 – Silk White	$14.99		
Cash In Cash Out – Assa Raymond Baker	$14.99		
Cash In Cash Out 2 - Assa Raymond Baker	$14.99		
Childhood Sweethearts – Jacob Spears	$14.99		
Childhood Sweethearts 2 – Jacob Spears	$14.99		
Childhood Sweethearts 3 - Jacob Spears	$14.99		
Childhood Sweethearts 4 - Jacob Spears	$14.99		
Connected To The Plug – Dwan Marquis Williams	$14.99		
Connected To The Plug 2 – Dwan Marquis Williams	$14.99		
Connected To The Plug 3 – Dwan Williams	$14.99		
Cost of Betrayal – W.C. Holloway	$14.99		
Cost of Betrayal 2 – W.C. Holloway	$14.99		
Deadly Reunion – Ernest Morris	$14.99		
Dream's Life – Assa Raymond Baker	$14.99		
Flipping Numbers – Ernest Morris	$14.99		

Flipping Numbers 2 – Ernest Morris	$14.99		
He Loves Me, He Loves You Not - Mychea	$14.99		
He Loves Me, He Loves You Not 2 - Mychea	$14.99		
He Loves Me, He Loves You Not 3 - Mychea	$14.99		
He Loves Me, He Loves You Not 4 – Mychea	$14.99		
He Loves Me, He Loves You Not 5 – Mychea	$14.99		
Killing Signs – Ernest Morris	$14.99		
Killing Signs 2 – Ernest Morris	$14.99		
Kings of the Block – Dwan Willams	$14.99		
Kings of the Block 2 – Dwan Willams	$14.99		
Lord of My Land – Jay Morrison	$14.99		
Lost and Turned Out – Ernest Morris	$14.99		
Love & Dedication – W.C. Holloway	$14.99		
Love Hates Violence – De'Wayne Maris	$14.99		
Love Hates Violence 2 – De'Wayne Maris	$14.99		
Love Hates Violence 3 – De'Wayne Maris	$14.99		
Love Hates Violence 4 – De'Wayne Maris	$14.99		
Married To Da Streets – Silk White	$14.99		
M.E.R.C. - Make Every Rep Count Health and Fitness	$14.99		
Mercenary In Love – J.L. Rose & J.L. Turner	$14.99		
Money Make Me Cum – Ernest Morris	$14.99		
My Besties – Asia Hill	$14.99		
My Besties 2 – Asia Hill	$14.99		
My Besties 3 – Asia Hill	$14.99		
My Besties 4 – Asia Hill	$14.99		
My Boyfriend's Wife - Mychea	$14.99		
My Boyfriend's Wife 2 – Mychea	$14.99		
My Brothers Envy – J. L. Rose	$14.99		
My Brothers Envy 2 – J. L. Rose	$14.99		
Naughty Housewives – Ernest Morris	$14.99		
Naughty Housewives 2 – Ernest Morris	$14.99		
Naughty Housewives 3 – Ernest Morris	$14.99		
Naughty Housewives 4 – Ernest Morris	$14.99		
Never Be The Same – Silk White	$14.99		
Scarred Faces – Assa Raymond Baker	$14.99		

Scarred Knuckles – Assa Raymond Baker	$14.99		
Shades of Revenge – Assa Raymond Baker	$14.99		
Slumped – Jason Brent	$14.99		
Someone's Gonna Get It – Mychea	$14.99		
Stranded – Silk White	$14.99		
Supreme & Justice – Ernest Morris	$14.99		
Supreme & Justice 2 – Ernest Morris	$14.99		
Supreme & Justice 3 – Ernest Morris	$14.99		
Tears of a Hustler - Silk White	$14.99		
Tears of a Hustler 2 - Silk White	$14.99		
Tears of a Hustler 3 - Silk White	$14.99		
Tears of a Hustler 4- Silk White	$14.99		
Tears of a Hustler 5 – Silk White	$14.99		
Tears of a Hustler 6 – Silk White	$14.99		
The Last Love Letter – Warren Holloway	$14.99		
The Last Love Letter 2 – Warren Holloway	$14.99		
The Panty Ripper - Reality Way	$14.99		
The Panty Ripper 3 – Reality Way	$14.99		
The Solution – Jay Morrison	$14.99		
The Teflon Queen – Silk White	$14.99		
The Teflon Queen 2 – Silk White	$14.99		
The Teflon Queen 3 – Silk White	$14.99		
The Teflon Queen 4 – Silk White	$14.99		
The Teflon Queen 5 – Silk White	$14.99		
The Teflon Queen 6 - Silk White	$14.99		
The Vacation – Silk White	$14.99		
Tied To A Boss - J.L. Rose	$14.99		
Tied To A Boss 2 - J.L. Rose	$14.99		
Tied To A Boss 3 - J.L. Rose	$14.99		
Tied To A Boss 4 - J.L. Rose	$14.99		
Tied To A Boss 5 - J.L. Rose	$14.99		
Time Is Money - Silk White	$14.99		
Tomorrow's Not Promised – Robert Torres	$14.99		
Tomorrow's Not Promised 2 – Robert Torres	$14.99		
Two Mask One Heart – Jacob Spears and Trayvon Jackson	$14.99		
Two Mask One Heart 2 – Jacob Spears and Trayvon Jackson	$14.99		

Two Mask One Heart 3 – Jacob Spears and Trayvon Jackson	$14.99		
Wrong Place Wrong Time – Silk White	$14.99		
Young Goonz – Reality Way	$14.99		
Subtotal:			
Tax:			
Shipping (Free) U.S. Media Mail:			
Total:			

Make Checks Payable To: Good2Go Publishing, 7311 W Glass Lane, Laveen, AZ 85339

CPSIA information can be obtained
at www.ICGtesting.com
Printed in the USA
LVHW082151140220
647003LV00012B/286

9 781947 340480